A BEAUTIFUL YOUNG WIFE

Tommy Wieringa was born in 1967, and grew up partly in the Netherlands and partly in the tropics. He began his writing career with travel stories and journalism, and is the author of five other novels. His fiction has been shortlisted for the International IMPAC Dublin Literary Award and the Oxford/ Weidenfeld Prize, and has won Holland's Libris Literature Prize.

Sam Garrett has translated some 40 novels and works of non-fiction. He has won prizes and appeared on shortlists for some of the world's most prestigious literary awards, and is the only translator to have twice won the British Society of Authors' Vondel Prize for Dutch-English translation.

For my brothers in arms: who else?

A Beautiful Young Wife

TOMMY WIERINGA

Translated from the Dutch by Sam Garrett

SCRIBE

Melbourne • London

Scribe Publications
18–20 Edward St, Brunswick, Victoria 3056, Australia
2 John Street, London, WC1N 2ES, United Kingdom

Originally published in Dutch by De Bezige Bij as
Een Mooie Jonge Vrouw 2014
First published in English by Scribe 2016

The publisher gratefully
acknowledges the support of the
Dutch Foundation for Literature.

N **ederlands**
letterenfonds
dutch foundation
for literature

Cover design by Jenny Grigg
Typeset in Adobe Caslon Pro by the publishers
Printed and bound in the UK by CPI Group (UK) Ltd, Croydon CR0 4YY

Scribe Publications is committed to the sustainable use of natural resources
and the use of paper products made responsibly from those resources.

9781925228410 (UK hardback)
9781925321180 (Australian paperback)
9781925307276 (e-book)

CiP records for this title are available from the British Library and the
National Library of Australia

scribepublications.com.au
scribepublications.co.uk

It's a pastime with which men and women entertain each other at dinner—couples who don't yet know each other well. The question is: 'How did you two meet, anyway?'

They look at each other. She says: 'You tell it. You're better at that.'

He starts in. 'Long ago, in a far-distant land …'

'That's not true! It was downtown Utrecht, seven years ago.'

'Okay, forget the fairytale.' He seems a bit disappointed. 'Utrecht, seven years ago. I'm sitting at this sidewalk café, and a girl comes bicycling down the street. She's not allowed to be riding a bike there at all, but this is the girl who's allowed to do anything—the girl to whom policemen show leniency, just this once, and who brings all traffic to a standstill.'

'You're exaggerating, sweetheart. And I was twenty-seven by then. Or twenty-eight.'

'She's riding a mountain bike, bent over a little, with her butt up in the air. I can't tell it without that detail, the butt that started everything. She rolled past me, down that crowded street, with her blonde hair and that butt …'

'All right already.'

1

'You wanted *me* to tell it, right?'

The other man at the table sits up straight. 'I want to hear about it, too. About that butt.'

'Lou! Control yourself,' his wife says.

'I saw her disappear into the crowd and I thought: *How am I ever going to find her again?* You know what that's like, Lou, you know what I'm talking about. That you feel like running after her and shouting: *Who are you? I can't live without you! Marry me, here, right now!*

'Hmm …' Lou says.

'Anyway, a few weeks later I was at the Willem I, and there she was again, at the pool table. That feeling, like it was in the cards: I found her again … without even looking. This is how it's supposed to be. She was playing pool with a girlfriend. With that butt again, like this … sticking up in the air …'

'Ed, please.'

'I went over to her and asked her name. I didn't want to let her get away again. She told me, sure, her name, but not where she lived. She wouldn't do that.'

'You were drunk.'

'But you told him your name, just like that?!' the other woman says.

'Why not?'

'A complete stranger?'

'I thought he was cute. Old, but cute.'

'*Old, but cute* …' Edward feigns a pain that is real.

2

'Older than I was. Are you happy now?'

'Fourteen years …'

'Plus one.'

'You want me to finish the story, or not?'

How he'd asked the barman for the phonebook, flipped through it, then tore out a page and took it over to her. She was lining up a shot in the corner pocket when he asked: 'Is this you?' He held the page beneath the lamp over the pool table and pointed to a name. She had looked Edward up and down in amusement. 'Could be,' she said.

'That's good, Ruth Walta. That's great. Thank you very much. I'm going to send you an invitation.'

'I'll wait and see,' she said. 'And what did you say your name was again?'

'Edward,' he said happily. 'Edward Landauer.'

'Hats off, Ed,' Lou says. 'That was a great move, that bit with the phonebook. That's real chutzpah.' He picks up the bottle and surveys the glasses. He tops up only Edward's glass.

'An act of desperation,' Edward says. 'I really didn't know what I would do without her. Imagine: a few minutes before all this happened, the world was still full of women, but now there was only her.' He smiles at his wife; his lips are purple. 'As though you have precisely one chance — fuck that one up, and the gates slam shut and the miracle will never repeat itself.' His forehead gleams; with his hands, he conducts the words above the tabletop.

'Didn't you find it a little scary, Ruth?' the other woman asks.

'It's so funny that you'd think that. It's nice to be overwhelmed a little, isn't it? A man who knows what he wants, who goes for the mark and all that, that's what we want, isn't it?'

'Yes, maybe it is …' She gets up. 'Lou, could you clear the table? And please, keep your knives and forks.'

In the kitchen, she slips on the oven gloves. That afternoon, in a shop selling Turkish and Surinamese specialties, she had picked up a bundle of okra and examined it. 'Keep both feet on the ground, Claudia,' Lou had said.

'But they're vegetarians! What am I supposed to do?'

What she did was potatoes au gratin, with vegetables from the grill.

Back at the table, Lou asks: 'Ruth, you noticed that he was older. But what about you, Ed? Did you see that she was younger?'

'No talking until I come back, you guys!' says a voice from the kitchen.

Edward closes his eyes for a moment—the girl holding the cue, the cigarette smoke rising and falling beneath the lamp above the table. He had always been powerless in the face of beauty. Dumbstruck. The solar disc between the horns of that faultless little Apis bull long ago in a museum in Damascus — someone had made that, dizzyingly long ago, hands like his had cast the bronze so perfectly. Gradually it had started dawning on him that beauty, too, could inflict pain, beauty above all; the way it could cut with light.

He opens his eyes. His beautiful young wife. 'No,' he says, 'not right away.'

'You didn't?'

'All I saw was … beauty, really. With no age attached.' He raises his glass.

She places her hand on his. 'Sweetheart …'

The hostess comes in, carrying a casserole. 'You were going to clear the dishes.'

'Right away,' Lou says.

She goes back to the kitchen and returns. No one offers to help.

'Delicious, Claudia,' Edward says a little later, raising his glass to her.

'Yes, honey, you got it just right,' Lou says.

'It was *made* right.'

'That's what I said.' He winks at Edward.

'And how did the rest of it go?' Claudia asks. 'Your getting to know each other?'

• • •

5

The evening after he came up and talked to her in the café, she typed his name into the search box. She saw pictures of him at international gatherings—he was apparently some bigwig in virology. He was taller than the rest, and she thought a beard looked good on him. A few days later, there was an invitation in the mailbox, for an outing with the boat. That same day, she responded with a postcard.

He rowed. She sat on the little bench at the back of the boat. There was almost no current. Gradually, the fields turned to woods—old, tall trees, individuals with names of their own. As they went gliding between round, mossy banks, mansions shimmered behind the greenery. Private property, no mooring. He thought about the families with their mysterious names; they had not held up, their backs broken by the weight of all the possessions and history. The chronicles stood written in mould on the damp walls. Great lawyers and statesmen had stepped forward from their ranks, men who had shaped the nation and passed it along in good shape to the next generation. That permanency, that was over and done with. Their great-grandchildren had become bankers and writers, their lives dedicated only to themselves.

The greenery folded closed above their heads, the crowns shot with arrows of prismatic light. He rowed soundlessly. Where the oars disappeared into the water, there arose silky purls of black and silver. He had his shirtsleeves rolled up. She thought his arms were nice.

They slid back into daylight. On the shore, they spread a blanket and lifted their faces to the late sun. Behind them was a cherry orchard, covered in green netting. He unpacked the basket and she asked: 'Did you make all this yourself?'—little sandwiches, a salad, the dressing kept separate. 'I love purslane,' he said. 'It tastes the way earth smells.'

When they had eaten a bit, she said, 'Come on, let's go and buy some cherries.'

She was wearing a white-cotton dress, and her legs were tanned. At the entrance to the orchard, a woman in an apron was sitting in a little shelter. Edward bought half a kilo of cherries. They were crisp and sweet; the spring had been warm and dry. They walked back to the river, and spat the pits as far away as they could.

They drank wine and talked about her sociology study that wasn't going well, and about the trips he took, the conferences he attended. He looked at her. Did she realise that she was drinking a bone-dry Apremont, perfect for an occasion like this? She scratched her leg. White furrows appeared beneath her nails.

As darkness starts to fall, he is the first to climb into the boat. He reaches out to her. She seizes his hand, and takes a giant step. He rows back, the current stronger than he'd thought. In the darkness beneath the trees, he wants to stay right in midstream and correct as little as possible; it needs to be perfect.

'Wait a minute,' she says after a while. She leans forward and places her hand on his. He stops rowing. 'Hear that?' she whispers. 'So quiet … Not even a bird.' Only the drops falling from the oars. Just before they touch the bank, he brings the left oar alongside and lets it rest in the water. Standing up, she says: 'Permission to go ashore?' They clamber up onto the bank, and he ties the boat. She disappears between the tall, smooth trunks, her white hair fluorescent and enticing. A creature that brings misfortune to those who follow her song, deeper and deeper into the woods.

The English country garden belongs to the mansion further along, tucked away amid the trees. The windows are darkened; there is no sign of life. He'll buy it for her and look at it from a distance each day, by nightfall—an illuminated beehive. That's where he will live and make children with this glorious woman, one child for each room.

She excites him incredibly, but he doesn't want to ruin it by being too greedy, by revealing his desperate longing. More than ever, he realises now, being in love connects him with the boy he once was, with the first time, his mouth dry and his heart pounding, the first time of all first times that followed. He had never married and had never been with one woman for long; he had always remained a collector of first times. Now he is forty-two and knows for a fact that everything has gone the way it's gone only in order to bring him to this girl.

She laughs as she reappears among the trees, a light-footed, heathen goddess. 'This is such a wonderful place,' she says. She speaks rather softly, as though the trees and the grass might hear. When she stands on tiptoe and kisses him, he has the confusing feeling that she went into the woods to consult with others of her kind— nymphs like her, gathered around the black, reflecting pool.

They lie on the humid bed of grass and moss, and make love slowly, with the timidity of bodies not yet fully acquainted. *So soon, so soon,* a voice inside him says. Her willingness makes him dizzy with happiness, gives him a thrill at the back of his throat at the sight of her young body, a dash of light on the forest floor. Haste, hunger, creeps into his movements. He forgets all he knows; hurried as a boy, he licks her belly, her salty sex, in abandon, as though he has drunk too much. Later, when he drives into her and leans on his arms, she writhes beneath him. He thrusts into her, she laughs, and says, 'I wondered when you'd get there.' Her experience surprises him; he had forgotten that people her age already know everything.

Their bodies are covered by the green half-light.

Sweat grows cold, semen contracting on skin. She lies on her side, in the shelter of his arm, his hand resting on her buttocks. 'Too bad you don't smoke,' she says.

'I've been told,' he says, 'that artists feel like they're further along than their predecessors. That they look at their work and think they've outstripped history. A feeling of … liberation. And triumph.'

'Why do you say that?'

He grins. 'Liberation and triumph.'

She's silent for a moment. 'You mean, like now?'

'Now.'

'Such a nice guy,' she says. And, a little later: 'And what about the next part?'

'What part's that?'

'The part where it never gets any better than this?'

They row in darkness, back to the boat rental, to the pastures and wooded banks. And far away, against the horizon, are the black buildings of the university, tossed down amid the fields without moderation or plan. A part of his life takes place there. Behind them stand the towers of the academic hospital, made of pulsing light, like a casino in the desert—win some, lose some. They slide under a chain, and tie up at a dock near the office; the shutters have been lowered and padlocked. You can buy candy and soft drinks there; hanging on the wall is a map of the area's waterways.

• • •

This happened in a café at the park's edge. The barman put down a glass in front of her and said: 'From the gentleman over there.' He nodded towards the far side of the bar. Edward took the glass and emptied it in one go. A few times, in the first years they were together, a drink would suddenly be set down before her. Edward would knock back Kahlúa and Blue Curaçao, his eyes fixed on the motionless figures across the bar. It could have been a saloon in Tombstone, 1885: she was the only pretty woman around, and men would lay down their lives for her. He was prepared for the fact that he could be struck down at any moment.

He knew that special beauty drew other admirers, too, a mobilisation of passion, men with a sporadically aggressive need to be seen by her. To let her know: you're mistaken, it's not him, it's me, *me*.

She was used to it. There were men who acted like that, just as there were men who behaved with exaggerated courtliness.

Her beauty had not deformed her, he thought, not like other women he'd known. Intelligent, stunning women, but intelligence and beauty in one and the same creature seemed to cause a deep inner disunity. It always took a while to see it, but after that you could never not see it again. Literature loved to portray such women as tragic heroines but, when he read about them, what he wished them most of all was a stringent regime of psycho-pharmaceuticals. In real life, he remained enthralled as long as they were able to hide their split nature. They were above-average in everything—in company no one was livelier, and in bed they were sensational, the world was their stage. But one by one they slipped out of character, sooner or later; the entrée of the tragic.

Ruth Walta seemed the lucky exception. He discovered no hidden chambers.

She said: 'I think I don't have all that many issues …'

'Issues …?'

'Women have issues.'

'And you don't?'

She shrugged. 'The usual female things, but otherwise nothing mysterious, I don't think. I hope that's not too boring for you?'

She had only a few girlfriends, and he considered that a good sign. Girlfriends sooner or later turned into a conspiracy—he remembered how they would go to the ladies' room together, their secret domain; after they came back, his position always felt compromised.

During their first summer together, she invited Henri and Diederik to their house: two friends she had met during her freshman year at college.

12

'You have a lovely place here, Mr. Landauer,' Henri said.

Edward grimaced. 'Please, call me Edward.'

Ruth came into the kitchen for an ashtray. He couldn't find one. In the doorway she turned, a saucer in her hand. 'Can I help with anything?'

'I'm almost done. Just go out and entertain them.'

From the garden, their voices sounded like those of passing cyclists. Had she done it with one of them? If so, then it must have been with Diederik. He had a broad, shapeless mouth, but the body of a water polo player. He had given Edward a powerful handshake. That's what it was all about, how you enfolded the other person's hand in yours; some handshakes were in equilibrium, but you also had those where your hand landed awkwardly in the other's, so you could apply no counter-pressure. There was no undoing it, you couldn't withdraw your hand and start all over again; you were under the other's sway. The boy's strong hand had taken him unawares.

He arranged scallops on a bed of chard, and took the plates to the dining room.

Ruth and Henri were outside, cocooned in the late-evening light. Wine and cigarettes and her sunglasses were on the table. Diederik was standing away from them, a bottle of beer in hand. What was he seeing? Peat-moss paths between the borders, pergolas of rose and passion flower. Edward stood between the sliding doors to the

13

garden. He removed his apron and said: 'Dinner's ready.'

'Let's eat outside,' Ruth said. 'It's lovely here.'

'It's going to get colder soon.'

'We won't be that long,' Ruth said. She stood up. Edward went inside, taking the plates from the table.

'Wait, Mr. Landauer, let me help,' Henri said.

Behind Ruth and Diederik, the sun went down. Diederik stuck a whole scallop in his mouth. *He doesn't even chew*, Edward thought. It could just as well have been a hamburger, for all he cared. He probably would have enjoyed that more.

Henri had tickets for a dance party. He'd ordered a few extra, so they could both go along if they liked. 'Fantastic,' Ruth said, but Edward shook his head. He remembered the parties of the 1980s, how everything went on and on, and how morning came with a mouth full of grit. He wasn't familiar with the music and drugs that were prevalent these days. That life had passed away; now he went to cafés, places where you could hear each other speak.

Henri asked about his job. 'Of course I know who you are, Mr. Landauer, but —'

'Please, call me Edward.'

Ruth laughed.

'I saw you on the news once,' the boy said, 'but I don't really know exactly what you do.'

Edward told him about his virus research. He had

14

just come back from a World Health Organisation mission to Hong Kong. All the poultry had been culled; the sky had turned black.

'Couldn't you be infected yourself now? How does that work?' Diederik asked.

'H5N1 doesn't transmit to humans,' Edward said. 'But influenza viruses mutate like lightning. So, who knows, at this very moment, somewhere in my lungs ...'

He longed to be alone with her. The boys were an intrusion. Through their eyes, he saw what the two of them were: a young woman with a much older man, a forty-two-year-old man of whom they asked, 'Are you still planning to have children?'

And Ruth, does she want children? Edward wondered. The subject had never come up. They'd been together for such a short time.

• • •

One day in late January, they drove across the big Zuyderzee causeway to a place in Friesland called Bozum, and pulled up by a newly built house at the edge of the village. Her father's silver Mercedes was in the carport. The back of the house faced onto pastureland that was vacant and glistening. This was where she had grown up. A life without major breakage — prosperity and the influx of information had burgeoned steadily

15

here, just like everywhere else, but life had retained its pastoral quality.

They were standing on the sun porch. He saw a spire in the distance—a vanishing point between the soft grey of the sky and the monotony of the grassland below.

'Look, a hare,' Edward said.

'Plenty of those around here,' said her father, from where he was sitting behind him.

He was a contractor—he had built the house himself. He took a cigarette from the dice cup on the table, ticked the filter against his thumbnail a few times, and lit it with a flame he cupped in his hand. A man acquainted with wind and rain. Edward remembered how, on a few occasions, his grandfather had offered him a cigarette from a cup like that. He was proud then that the old man had viewed him as the kind of fellow who smoked.

Her father leaned forward in his easy chair, elbows resting on his thighs, his head hunched down a bit between his shoulders; a labourer during his break.

They drank coffee from fragile porcelain cups. 'Do you use milk?' the mother asked. His coffee went white from the dash of condensed.

'They're called *Fryske dúmkes* [hazelnut and aniseed biscuits],' the mother said. 'Ever had them before?'

Try as she might, the echo of Frisian rang from every word. He shook his head, his mouth full of cookie.

Later, Ruth and her mother disappeared upstairs to sort things out—what could be disposed of, what could not.

Edward looked at the photos on the dresser: Ruth as a child, a creature woven of light and gold filigree; riding a horse, petting the powerful neck of a bull in some farmyard; smiling into the camera with big, strong teeth, her little brother on her back.

Her father came and stood beside him, a bottle of aged gin and two glasses in his hand. 'The old clock on the wall has almost reached five. You do drink now, don't you?' He poured for both of them. '*Tsjoch*, that's what we say around these parts. Do you know what that means?'

'Cheers, I guess?'

'Exactly.'

'*Tsjoch*,' Edward said.

'*Tsjoch*.'

They drank. Her father tapped his index finger against one of the photos. 'Do you know who that is?'

Edward looked. 'Ruth?'

'No, this fella here.'

Edward moved his face up closer, trying to look as though he might know something about cattle. 'No idea,' he said at last.

'Sunny Boy. Still a young one then, not nearly the champion he became a few years later. But what a power he had in that body already … A million offspring, no less.'

A pair of champions, the bull and the girl. The animal was awesome, but Edward couldn't stop looking at Ruth. She was barely twelve, thirteen. Even back then, he would have desired her desperately.

'And what plans do you have, if you don't mind my asking?' her father said with a force that made it seem as though he'd been holding back till then. He was shorter than Edward, but with the immovability of a wrestler. He had broad, strong fingers with cracks that had never come completely clean.

'Plans?' Edward said.

'With Ruth. You're a bit older, if I'm correct.'

Edward wondered about the connection between the question concerning his plans and the stud bull her father had just pointed out to him. 'There's a few years' difference, yes,' he said. 'It's not ideal, but … I regret that I had to turn forty before meeting her …'

'Forty-two, that's what she said.'

A hot glow spread up towards his ears.

'You could have had a family of your own already.'

Edward stood up straight. 'I could have. But I didn't.'

'You know that she's been married before?'

Dizziness.

'You didn't know that?'

His alarm-red thought: the secret chamber … he had

found it. 'No,' Edward said, 'no, I didn't know that.'

'It was right after she moved away from home.'

They were making a fool of him, the father and the daughter. They were laughing, laughing.

'I asked her whether she had a good reason for getting married. Love, she said. That's not an answer, I said. He was a good boy, for sure, but he had never done an honest day's work in his life. She'd never been so in love before, she said. When she came back from America, she showed us the ring. It was a surprise …'

'A surprise. Indeed.'

'We puzzled over it and puzzled over it, but never did understand why she had to go and do that.' He sighed. 'She never has let anyone tell her what to do.' He tipped the second glass into his mouth and said, his lips wet: 'You and me are ten years apart. You're more like my own generation. I had hoped that she would take care of me someday, but the way things look now, it'll be your wheelchair she's pushing. Is that what you want, to have my daughter be your nurse?'

'It's … it's maybe a little too early to think about that yet.'

'Oh, is that what you figure? Listen, let me tell your fortune for you, right down to the year. Ten years from now, some doctor will have already stuck his finger up you twice, to check your prostate. That hurts. You'll already have been on one of those bicycles to measure your heart functions, after you felt that tingling spread down to your fingers. And the plumbing's getting a bit rusty, too. To read the little information leaflet, you're going to need your glasses. But where did you leave the damn things?'

Edward smiled. Her father was a humourist, he was sure of that now.

'There,' he said. He pointed at Edward's forehead.

Edward didn't get it.

'There they are, on your forehead!'

Edward ran his hand through his hair. 'What?'

'Your glasses! Your reading glasses!'

'I still get along fine without them,' Edward said, when the other man was finished laughing.

'Talk to me again in three years' time.'

'We'll see.'

'Oh, we will indeed.' He slapped him on the shoulder.

After supper, he and Ruth took a walk around the village. At the edge of Bozum, in the dark, was the church. 'It's really old,' Ruth said, her eyes fixed on the building. 'I don't even know exactly how old.'

The gate was open. They walked along a gravel path between the headstones.

'Your father shouldn't have been the one to tell me,' he said bluntly.

They stopped, little stones gnashing beneath their

soles. She didn't know what he meant.

'About your having been married,' he said.

'Oh no, not ...'

He ground little potholes with his heels. 'It was painful.'

'I was meaning to tell you myself.'

The clock at the top of the tower struck the half hour.

'It was no big deal, really. We went to Las Vegas — he'd been wearing cowboy boots since he was thirteen, for the day when he would drive into Vegas in a Chevrolet. Then we saw one of those little chapels ... Well, that was it, really.'

He shoved his hands into his pockets and walked on.

'I'm sorry, love, that you had to hear about it this way,' she said from behind him.

Behind the church was a gravedigger's hut. The door was open, so he ducked down and looked inside. In the semi-darkness he made out a few pallbearer's poles and partitions they used to shore up the walls of the graves. He pulled Ruth inside and pushed her up against the wall; his hands disappeared under her sweater and grasped her little breasts. Gooseflesh. They did it standing against the wall; she breathed heavily against his neck. He fucked her hard and punishingly. With his ejaculation, he vanquished the man with the cowboy boots, and the father, too, and carried her away from there. The bull with the girl on its back.

*

When Edward Landauer was seventeen and had to decide what he was going to study, he saw two possibilities. He could either peer into the cosmos through a telescope, in search of new life, of moons and meteorites with grit in their tails, or he could bend over microscopes to study the fundaments of human life. In a youth hostel in Copenhagen, he read *Thus Spoke Zarathustra*, and found the answer in Nietzsche's impassioned summons to remain faithful to the earth.

In those days, medical microbiology was a fairly ho-hum field. The smallpox virus had been eliminated, tuberculosis no longer played a significant role in the Western world, and the polio vaccine was almost 100 per cent effective. The battle seemed over. What was left now were the residual illnesses, viruses and bacteria still rampant in the Third World, and Edward was prepared to dedicate his research life to those.

Then, in 1981, a man in Amsterdam died from a mysterious stack of nasty diseases. 'Patient Zero' was a strong, healthy man who had been destroyed in a trice by a muddle of immune sicknesses. Almost every specialist in the hospital was at his bedside, but they were powerless to help him.

In January 1983, three more patients were admitted with the same symptoms; a few months later, seven more. Before the year was over, most of them had died.

Their immune systems were out of whack; opportunistic infections had destroyed their bodies. They served as staging grounds for a proliferation of viruses and fungi, of aggressive skin cancers and neurological ailments affecting the brain and spinal cord. They went blind and senile, and drowned in their own fluids. No one knew what kind of disease this was or where it had come from. The only apparent correlative was that it seemed to strike mostly homosexual men, men with an often highly promiscuous sex life — some of the respondents reported having hundreds of sex partners each year.

Edward heard someone in the hospital refer to it as 'homo-cancer', but it soon became clear that haemophilia patients, drug addicts, and recipients of blood transfusions were also susceptible. The disease took on a name, 'Acquired Immune Deficiency Syndrome', otherwise known as AIDS.

Edward was twenty-five, his thesis written in the company of those researching the new disease. That was how he came to be given an internship with virology professor Herman Wigboldus. Wigboldus, the story was legendary, had brought the isolated AIDS virus back from America in his breast pocket. As if by magic, he had transformed the sleepy field of medical microbiology into the frontline of modern science, and Edward, by a stroke of good luck, was right in the thick of it. There was money, prestige, and fame to be had. That was the glorious side of it: the epoch-making research, the thrill of the new, the pioneering work. People called them the cowboys of AIDS research.

The other end of the spectrum was marked by fear and despair. There were surgeons who, fearing infection, refused to operate on homosexual males. No one knew how the virus spread. Anything was possible: airborne contact, sexual contact, or even the toilet seat. One female lab assistant quickly developed an acute form of nosophobia and panicked at the pipettes containing virus material. Wigboldus, when he came into the lab, would sometimes roar 'Virus!,' and everyone would laugh as she froze on her stool. She finished her internship at the veterinary faculty of the University of Utrecht.

Edward lived in a whirl of excitement. Patients were dying en masse; scientific research was being carried out with warlike urgency. Laboratory staffers organised information evenings in meeting rooms filled with terrified homosexual men. 'Dr. Landauer, my partner is HIV positive, and so am I. Should we be using condoms?'

Questions to which there were no answers.

During a departmental meeting, Wigboldus told them: 'It looks like we're going to have to say sorry to the entire first and second generations.'

The lab assistants were silent. 'What do you mean, "sorry"?' one of the researchers asked at last.

'Just that,' Wigboldus said. 'They're all doomed.'

One autumn day, Edward was in the canteen, watching an anti-nuclear march in The Hague on the little TV there. As hordes of people shuffled past, the reporter said it could very well develop into the largest protest demonstration ever held in the Netherlands.

A man came up and stood beside Edward. For a while, the two of them watched the live broadcast from Malieveld. 'The fools,' the man said then. 'What they don't realise is that viruses are what's going to kill them, not atom bombs.'

Under Wigboldus' forceful leadership, some seven interns and post-docs were kneaded into serviceable material. They published in *Nature*, *Science*, and *The Lancet*: the flow of research funding was endless. Edward went along to conferences, and learned from Wigboldus about who hated whom, and with whom he would do well to forge coalitions. 'You need to understand the way the game is played,' Wigboldus said. 'That, combined with brilliant research — and we'll pipette us together a Nobel Prize yet, my boy.'

He sounded like a used-car salesman, Edward thought, yet he understood that Wigboldus' pugnacity and lack of scruples were the building blocks of his success.

'Science is the destruction of reputations,' his mentor told him one evening in a hotel bar. 'Creative destruction. Scuttling other people's careers when your study knocks theirs for a loop.' The glee in his voice was unmissable.

It was within this culture of dedicated pioneering and power lust that Edward was formed. Wigboldus' hunkering for glory was fused seamlessly to the public interest; Edward had seen him profess great commitment to his patients while, once beyond range of the cameras, he granted much higher priority to cutting the National Institutes of Health or the Institut Pasteur off at the pass.

Wigboldus' authoritarian behaviour didn't intimidate Edward. He knew the man valued him for his scientific intuition. In addition, Edward possessed a gift for clearly and simply explaining the state of affairs in their field of research, so that Wigboldus could leave most of the media contacts to him. And because the dynamic field surrounding the new retrovirus also included an element of hysteria, there was something to explain or comment on each week.

Wigboldus lived with his wife and two dogs in a villa at the edge of Amstelveen. When Edward was invited over for dinner one time and crossed the lawn on his way to the front door, Wigboldus asked him to wipe his feet on the grass. 'That keeps some of the filth of the city outside.'

For an internationally celebrated virologist, Edward thought, this was a puzzling and highly unscientific train of thought. He wrote it off to eccentricity. The couple's dalmatians lay on the easy chairs and were fed scraps from the dining-room table. He had never dared to ask why they had no children.

One day, Edward walked into Wigboldus' office. 'Herman, there's something I need your help with,' he said.

In some human cell cultures, he had observed divergent effects on the infection, confirming his hunch that there were actually two types of virus. They worked out the hypothesis and systematically isolated viruses from a large patient group. As it turned out, one of the HIV variants destroyed the patient more quickly than the other did. No one had ever suspected this before: he was the first.

Bottles of champagne were taken out of the lab coolers, and the festive atmosphere hung in the air for days. Edward obtained his doctorate with a thesis on his discovery; he also published four articles about it in *Science* and *The Lancet*, and took a giant step up the hierarchical ladder. From being the most junior research assistant, he was promoted to Wigboldus' sorcerer's apprentice.

His flash of intuition had been a moment of receptiveness, a rare moment of illumination—because he practised science by feel, like a diver in murky waters.

Occasionally he stopped and thought about the turn his life had taken. From being a dependable lab rat, he had become a person of importance, a man whose face was seen in the world. All thanks to a micro-organism made of protein and nucleic acid, too small to be viewed through anything but an electron microscope. The whole world was talking about it, but he was one of the few who had ever seen it in real life.

In their publications, Wigboldus was almost always cited as the principal author, even for those studies Edward had devised himself, yet he tolerated this tacitly; a form of mutualism had developed between them that he had no desire to disturb with displays of hurt pride.

It was at a conference in Berlin that Edward first noted a certain war-weariness. It was 1993, and there was still no prospect of a course of treatment, no sign of the magic bullet that would stop the virus. Ten years of research had produced minor improvements, but for most patients the illness was still deadly. It took three more years, until combination therapy was introduced, for AIDS to gradually become a chronic ailment.

Sometimes he thought back fondly on the early days of AIDS research; the creativity and hunger of that time, it seemed, had disappeared—not only for him, but for the entire field.

Somewhere back there, amid the turbulence, his mother had died, too. It was only witnessing his father's sorrow that finally brought on the tears. He was back at work the day after the funeral.

Missing her arrived in little fits and starts, as sudden realisations of the void at the edge of his life—the questions he could no longer ask, the comfort of her hand on the back of his neck, her warm pride that had always enveloped him, no matter what he did. Sometimes he caught himself thinking: *You can come back now, Mum. It's lasted long enough.*

Herman Wigboldus was the first who dared to admit that the thrill was gone. They were sitting in a Japanese restaurant, the sashimi served beneath a dome of ice. Wigboldus tapped a hole in it and shattered the rest of the dome with his chopsticks. 'Unusual, this,' he mumbled.

He ate hastily, like a conqueror.

Without looking up from his plate, he told Edward that he was thinking about quitting. AIDS had become a pharmaceutical problem; there was no longer any cause for fundamental research. He'd received an offer to develop vaccines for a publicly listed biotechnology firm, and it seemed like a good moment to make the switch.

Mammon beckons, Edward thought. Wigboldus had

always been interested in money, and now that he was nearing fifty he saw his chance to make a bundle. Edward understood that the older man's outpouring was meant to encourage him not to hang around any longer either, there where they had already skimmed off the creamiest of the cream.

• • •

His future came to him on the wings of a bird. In 1997, eighteen people in Hong Kong fell ill after contracting an avian influenza of the type H5N1. Six of them died —one in three. By way of comparison, the Spanish Flu had killed approximately one in forty. The alarm was heard around the world. For the first time, an avian flu had shown itself transferrable directly to humans, without what had previously been seen as the requisite interim host, the pig. It looked like a catastrophe was on its way, but no one could predict whether it would claim six victims or sixty million. Some two million poultry birds were culled in the Hong Kong region alone.

That was the start. Change was in the air.

Edward made an appointment with Jaap Gerson, director of the Centre for Infectious Disease Control in Bilthoven. On his way to their meeting place at the hotel-restaurant beside the A1 highway, he thought about what Wigboldus had said: 'The moment has slipped away. The originality has worn off. We have to re-invent ourselves, Ed, find something new. Be opportunistic. No need to be ashamed of that. Opportunism is good.'

Even before their gravy rolls and bread arrived, Jaap Gerson said: 'I've always got room for someone like you.'

Edward said: 'Remember that big demonstration in The Hague? I was watching TV in the canteen when you came and stood beside me. You said something I've never forgotten. Something along the lines of our not being destroyed by nuclear weapons, but by viruses.'

Gerson nodded. 'I guess I could have said something just like that.'

For almost a year, Edward drove back and forth between Amsterdam and Bilthoven. Then he moved to Utrecht, to a house with a garden beside Wilhelmina Park. He furnished it sparsely; when he came home in the evening, he sometimes had the feeling he was visiting a stranger. When he looked at the lives others led, he felt envious of their comfortable homes and their loves, the children they had. From that moment on, they formed closed units, focusing on themselves, their backs half-turned to the world. You lost them for a long time. Some of them you never got back at all.

In 1999, he was appointed head of the Laboratory for Zoonoses and Environmental Microbiology, and was offered a named professorship, allowing him to deliver weekly lectures at the University of Utrecht on *The microbiological drivers for zoonosis emergence.*

His calling card said PROF. DR. EDWARD LANDAUER, but he still lived like a leaf blown by the wind. His life could just as easily have been taking place in Frankfurt or Singapore. There were women, encounters in semi-darkness, phrases at the café door that made the difference: 'There are three things we can do: your place, my place, or each of us to their own place. You get to choose between the first two.'

He was proficient at it, but found himself no longer suited to that endless student's life. How he was to go about changing it, though, he had no idea.

One day, when a girl bicycled past the sidewalk café where he was having coffee, he realised what he was missing. Long after she had disappeared into the crowd, and the stab of desire had ebbed away, he also experienced something new: an acute sense of missing someone he didn't know yet, from far beyond the storms of infatuation and the perilous years of marriage, as though looking back out of old age at a love that had been broken off abruptly. It gave him a hint of the extent of his capacity for love. It was among the moments he would never forget. The image of the girl on her bicycle contained everything, like the DNA of the micro-organisms sent to him from all over the world, but was nevertheless immeasurably light, a gleaming bubble that floated silently through time and that he could summon up whenever and wherever he liked.

• • •

As soon as the opportunity arose, he took Ruth along to a medical ski conference in Aspen. The driver waiting for them at the airport held aloft a sign. MR. & MRS. LANDAUER. A little later, Ruth was standing at the window of their hotel room, looking out over the silent white mountains. Edward lay on the bed, his hands folded behind his head, happy as a gangster who has just covered his moll beneath a flurry of banknotes.

She turned. 'Who's paying for all of this?'

'GlaxoSmithKline,' he said.

She looked outside again. 'We don't have a clue,' she said to the glass. 'We really don't have a clue.'

In the morning, he attended lectures and mingled with old acquaintances. Speakers appeared wearing their ski outfits. The last speaker of the day already had his goggles pushed up on his forehead and said: 'Ladies and gentlemen, I'm going to keep it brief, because of course you all want to get out on the slopes as quickly as possible …' Laughter came from a thousand throats.

Edward and Ruth brunched on waffles with maple syrup, blueberries, and poached eggs, and didn't take the chairlift up until far past noon. Neither of them could ski very well. His joints bothered him. After a few runs, in the chairlift again, she laid her head on his shoulder and said that something like this, this fantastic view, would have seemed impossible to her when she was little and growing up in Bozum, where mountain ranges sometimes appeared on the horizon — but those were landscapes of cloud that disappeared after a while, leaving you in that green vastness with only a steeple here and there.

Even back then, she told him that afternoon as they sat on the deck of the lodge with a valley view, the farmers had tended to keep their cows inside as much as possible, in the spring and summer, too — it was only the rare dairyman who put his cows out to pasture. They simply didn't care. But her vegetarianism, the decisive moment, only came after she had slept over at a girlfriend's house and heard the pigs being taken away in the middle of the night. Their screams as they were herded into the trucks were so unspeakably horrific that, that night, a deep awareness of the suffering of other species had been carved into her soul. An animal that screamed like that knew everything. It possessed a form of awareness of its fate, and experienced a fear, for which no comfort existed. She had understood that wordlessly. That night, a boundary between her and all other things living on this earth had been lifted, and once that happened there was no going back.

There was no distance between the little girl who felt sorrow at these things and the woman who related her memories to him in the snow.

Edward had heard the story before, with slight variations and additions, but he forgave her the repetition. He did his best to empathise with the life of the soul of a nine-year-old girl, but sometimes thought back with a twinge on things that had since vanished from his repertoire: the *scaloppine al limone*, and the lamb chops with a crust of breadcrumbs and parmesan, dishes with which he had impressed others.

A little more than two years ago, not long after they met, he had bought a few vegetarian cookbooks and adopted her dietary laws in the kitchen; she was resolute when it came to meat, but would eat shellfish by exception. One advantage was that, without even trying, he lost more than six kilos during their first six months together. The hope that he would lose even more weight turned out to be in vain, though; he continued to bob somewhere around 100 kilos, still a good eighteen kilos too much for a man his height.

Early on in her student days, Ruth had fixed macrobiotic meals in the common kitchen of a squat. When it turned out that she had no talent for cooking, though, she was quickly relegated to waiting on tables. A few times, they'd had friends from her old activist milieu over for dinner. Their vegetarianism had something barren and whiny about it, Edward thought, whereas hers seemed pure and noble.

By five that afternoon, they were back on the valley floor. Ruth went to the hotel, but he still had a few duties to perform. There was a poster session at the conference centre; snow still clinging to their shoes, gin-and-tonics in hand, the researchers strolled past the exhibits. Two young post-docs from his institute, the best of their batch, had arrived in Aspen the night before. The girl, unfortunately, was not very pretty; good looks always came in handy. Long ago, when he was still a teaching assistant, he had stood in front of a poster at the Amsterdam research institute with a hockey girl from Laren—flattered, but a bit offended for form's sake, she had said: 'I've been offered three internships in the space of two hours!'

Later in the evening, he and the post-docs walked from the conference centre to the hotel. The session had gone well, a man from a pharmaceuticals company had been enthusiastic about their method of promoting the efficient mutation of viruses, and there had been interest in the neutralising antibodies that could wipe out a whole group of viruses at a swoop. It was the only research project in which Edward still took part. The virus he was dealing with had originated in factory farming. Minor outbreaks had been reported, and the damage had remained limited—a few dead animals, potentially infected stock eliminated. The ways of the WHO and the Food and Agriculture Organisation were quick and efficient. Doing research reminded him of his own Amsterdam years, but to his regret it never assumed quite the same urgency as before. Maybe he was simply no longer capable of such fire; maybe his heart was slowly guttering and dying.

They were on their second round by the time Ruth came down to the hotel bar. She was wearing a Norwegian sweater and shiny white trousers. He still didn't feel, he realised, like she was really his. It was as though he hadn't won her heart, but had acquired her by theft. Something about her aroused a hunger in him, and excitement. There were women who never lost that, that sense of something blossoming and healthy. As they grew older, their blonde hair only shifted a few tints and they became grey-blonde, like Linda Evans in *Dynasty*. No one in this little group, he realised then, would have any idea who Linda Evans was. Their youth had known other celebrities.

'You should take a couple of lessons,' the male post-doc was telling Ruth. 'If you can't do it right away, you just pick yourself up and brush yourself off.'

'Literally, yes,' his female colleague said.

Edward didn't like seeing her with people her own age. It only exposed what had taken place in the time they'd been together: she had not made him younger, but because of him she had become older. In the company of her peers she took on her true age, light and sparkling, while he remained behind on his island in the distant future, grumbling through his whiskers.

• • •

Edward Landauer did not think back on his younger years very often, but he did hold a few vivid memories of the outings he'd made as a boy around his village. He had wandered down wooded lanes and across heaths, across the army shooting range and through the vast woods behind it. It was a landscape he remembered as being empty, as though there had been almost no other people, a world that seemed to have disappeared afterwards; a ship, sunken soundlessly on the horizon.

Occasionally he would come across a concrete carcass bin and open it with a yearning he didn't understand. The metal lids always had a counterweight, and stayed upright once you had opened them. He saw calves, lambs, and piglets, sometimes still enveloped in the placenta, and on rare occasions a foal—a Noah's Ark of the dead. He got lost in the pelagic void of their soft eyes. Maggots crawled from their mouths and anuses. Shivering with pleasure, he looked at the swellings and deformities, but sometimes the young animals were perfect and whole, and one couldn't see what they had died of. Something inside them had killed these perfect animals. A structural defect.

From time to time, whenever a highly pathogenic virus was haunting the stalls, he would think back on the carcass bins of yore—during an emergency session of the Food & Commodities Authority, for example, when he recommended the culling of livestock. Within a few days, thirty-five million chickens spread over ten square kilometres could vanish like that. The numbers staggered his imagination. A shed full of chicks, a rolling surface of teeming life; where the farmer walked, the sea parted. In sheds free of the virus, he had seen how farmers plucked sick and enfeebled birds from among the others and killed them with a pinch to the back of the neck. The whacking of the skull against the wooden shoe was just to be sure. They tossed them into buckets full of other dead chicks. Their arms had made that movement countless times before; they almost never missed. When the chicks became a bit larger, the farmer would pull a wheelbarrow behind him through the shed.

No one shed a tear for the chickens. When it came to pigs and cows, though, things were different. The apocalyptic images of men in white suits using a hydraulic claw to load dead heifers and sows into trucks were printed indelibly in people's minds.

Following an outbreak of an avian flu virus, all the

chickens were gassed, and badly paid and sketchily briefed students or asylum-seekers came in afterwards to clean up the sheds. The Rendac trucks had replaced the carcass bins. Death had vanished from the landscape, the way living animals had also quietly disappeared from it—they lived in increasingly great numbers in increasingly large stall complexes, and the speed with which they grew was stunning.

He couldn't avoid talking to Ruth about it at times, and when he did he withdrew behind the facts. Most of the epidemics, he said, began in Asia, because of the frequent contact there between humans and animals. There, one found ducks and chickens piled up at open-air markets. The chain of infection was easy to trace back. Ducks were often the carriers of viruses transmitted by their congeners in the wild, and they in turn infected the chickens. The Asian markets were crowded—little wonder that it was precisely there that the avian flu virus first hopped to humans. Along with the increasing urbanisation, and a billion instances of global travel each year, and you could see how a pandemic could get rolling within a matter of days. That was why chickens had to be bred under controlled conditions. Every step they took outside the shed was a risk, for the birds and for humans. Don't forget, he went on, that the Spanish Flu wiped out about 2 per cent of all mankind—for us, that would mean about three or four funerals each month.

Her objection was ironclad. If that's the way the world was, she said, then it shouldn't be. Capitalism and expansion were what had made it so ugly, and sometimes Ruth could not sleep at night, thinking that he was serving the interests of big industry.

He didn't like what he saw, he would reply. It was not beautiful and it was not good, but aesthetics and morality were not a part of his job. He only combatted the diseases that came from the world the way it was, in order to prevent worse.

'And what about the animals' pain?' she asked.

The naiveté of the question bowled him over.

He said: 'Humans are animals, too.'

'Pain is bad,' she said. 'You shouldn't do anything that increases the amount of pain in the world.'

While he was still trying to figure out whether a fight was brewing here, she said: 'Do you actually know what pain is? Real pain? I don't think you do, otherwise you couldn't walk through a stall like that without feeling anything.'

'So in order to understand the chicken's pain, you have to have experienced it yourself? What do you think the pain of a chicken is like?'

His question was meant to be sardonic without sounding sardonic. But when he thought back on the poultry sheds he had visited, fear and confusion were

41

indeed fairly accurate descriptions of the state in which the chickens found themselves.

• • •

There were portents: as he was reading a lab journal, Marjolein van Unen, an analyst who he found vaguely attractive, said: 'Before long, your arms will be too short for that.' Whenever he came in, she would take off her white lab coat; the T-shirts she wore were low-cut. His father-in-law's prophecy kept him from seeing an optician—he was forty-five now, so the prediction had proven accurate down to the very year. Ruth thought it was ridiculous, the way he kept bumping up the font on the screens of his phone and laptop, so she bought him a pair of oval reading glasses, the same frames that Schubert and Mörike had worn on the tips of their noses. The letters leapt up at him from the page, and he couldn't figure out why he had put up for so long with the haziness across the words.

Sometimes, while introducing a cotton swab with virus material into a ferret's throat, he remembered what Ruth had asked him: *Do you actually know what pain is?* How could you know whether your receptors were sensitive or insensitive to that? It was not a category that could be quantified. Pain could not be measured. It was an incomprehensible scientific omission, when he stopped to think about it. At lunchtime, he looked around the canteen and saw himself amid all the epidemiologists, immunologists, and virologists, a realist among the realists, all of them hired to maintain the status quo. Did they know what pain was? Could they bridge the gap between their own pain and the pain of the animals they worked with? He looked at the tray on which he'd assembled his lunch: a glass of milk and a gravy-roll sandwich (two times bovine pain), a banana (*banana* pain?), and a fricandeau sandwich. Pork fricandeau, he assumed. At one of the tables, he saw two analysts from his department.

'Hello, Hester. Hello, Marjolein,' he said. 'Do you mind if I sit with you while I eat my pig-pain sandwich?'

'Professor Dr. Landauer,' Marjolein van Unen said.

He caught the mockery. It was precisely her lack of blatant beauty that excited him. She had something available about her, like some of the girls in his native village of whom people said that they went along with everyone, back behind the church.

Twice a week, he went to the gym. For a while he had gone running in the park, but he couldn't stand the looks of the joggers who crossed his path. He was startled by the men who caught up with and passed him—their malicious snorting, the sweat pouring down their faces. You'd have goddamn thought they were coming to rob you.

43

In the gym, he saw the commercial broadcasts on TV screens suspended from the ceiling, and heard the inane pop songs blaring from the speakers. A silent procession of TV cooks and equities analysts marched across the screens, and newsreaders with their wan smiles. Only when a superior body entered his field of vision did he look up: the girl in calf-length leggings and her gorgeous buttocks, the black boy doing his stretching exercises with a studied nonchalance. The sight of a beautiful body shattered any positive thoughts he might have had about his own person; he tugged at the weights, feeling puny and worthless; in fact, all he wanted to do was to go home.

In the car, Edward comforted himself with the thought that, unlike the narcissistic homos with their gym-buffed bodies who he had seen go to pieces during his years in Amsterdam, he was still alive. But he knew how feeble this internal defence was, how meagre the consolation he derived from the fact that 'at least everything still works'.

Gone was his old sense of disassociation upon coming home. Ruth had attached herself to the house and made it theirs. The hallway and the downstairs bathroom had been painted in what she called 'Caribbean colours'. The bathroom windowsill was full of shells she'd collected from North Sea beaches; little piles of sand fell out of them.

'How can you live like this?' she'd said the first time she went home with him. She hardly listened to his objection that the chaise longue and the wood-and-leather stool were *design* objects.

She stood in front of his bookcase for a while, head tilted to one side, then said: 'Have you actually read all these books?'

'And remembered them,' he said.

His scanty household goods were gradually subsumed by the flood of things and doo-dads she brought in. She had her own study upstairs, where she finally completed her thesis, not out of any inspiration but from a sense of duty implanted in her by earlier generations. When she had started furnishing the room it had contained nothing—not one moving box or saggy chair. There was a possibility that he had actually been in that room once before, he figured, on the day the agent had shown him around the house. But, as he commented in reply to her amazement, there had never been a reason to go in there after that.

'Bluebeard's chamber,' she said, 'with nothing in it.'

In the meantime she had started working four days a week for a foundation that studied the financial behaviour of households, and she served as advisor to the Ministry of Social Affairs concerning the financial-economic situation of vulnerable groups. Once, they had both been on TV on the same evening, with her talking about hidden poverty among the elderly, and Edward discussing the threat of bio-terrorism. 'Par for the course,' she said. 'You on the commercial channel, and me on national public TV.'

Their trip to Aspen had revealed to her the closely knit interests of science and industry, and even though he tried to explain to her that things had to be that way, that otherwise all kinds of fundamental research could never be funded — his professorial chair, in fact, was also sponsored by Danone and GlaxoSmithKline — it did nothing to lessen her disgust. 'I believe you, it's not that,' she said. 'But it shouldn't be that way. It's not right. How can you be objective about that? What do they make anyway, pills?'

'Pills, all kinds of things.'

'You can't tell me that they're not expecting something in return for a vacation to the States like that.'

'It's been that way forever in the exact sciences,' he said. 'The researcher motivated by pure intellectual curiosity, standing with his back to the world, is a thing of the past. That's how it's been for a long time.'

'But that still doesn't answer my question.' She kicked off her shoes, which had something ominous about it under the circumstances.

'It's probably all very complex,' he said, 'but at the very start of the process, it's really quite simple. We try to solve problems, so that the doctor won't have to throw up his hands when you're bitten by a tick or when you've had unsafe sex in the Gambia.' He reached out to her. 'But now that I mention it, speaking of unsafe sex …'

'We're having a conversation, goddamn it.'

She had slipped into a polemical mood; he knew she would now defend her standpoint to beyond the borders of the reasonable.

'What do you want me to say?' he said. 'That I'm a pawn of the industry? Well, I'm not. Is there any danger of becoming one? Yes, there is. I know guys who push the limits, who even step over the boundaries at times, but that doesn't mean you can relegate everyone and everything to the same scrap heap, that —'

'As far as I could tell, everyone was at that conference. Everyone. Eating, drinking, skiing, a little networking and then back to eating, drinking, skiing …'

'Which is to say?'

'That you let yourself be pampered, too, like everyone else … the chauffeur, the welcome cocktail, the room …'

'Maybe what's bothering you is that you enjoyed it so much,' he said.

Ruth got up and went to the kitchen. He picked up his glass and went after her. She was staring out the window at the darkened garden. A lock of hair hung down over her face. 'You know,' she said, 'that was the first time I'd experienced something like that. I had no idea how seductive it could be. It was really very nice—

47

the food, the good wine, the mountains. I let myself be lulled to sleep. But now I understand how things like that work.' She turned her head to look at him. 'It was the last time I'll go along. I hope you realise that.'

Her anger had made way for something else, something resigned, but now the rage welled up in him. 'That's … uh …' He nodded, his eyes closed. The trips, the hotels with their wainscoting and mirrored walls, that was part of how he saw the life they were going to have together. Now it had made him a suspect. She saw the tightness around his jaw, she waited for the outburst, but when he opened his eyes the rage had worked its way out of his expression. Slowly, he said: 'Your neo-Marxist friends will be proud of you. But I am … not amused.'

That was it. He went no further. He climbed the stairs, leaving her behind in the kitchen, a woman unappeased; she poured herself the last sip of wine left in the bottle.

She had seen him keep himself in check; he couldn't hide the fact that he didn't dare to do otherwise. He couldn't remember ever letting himself go in an argument. He controlled himself, which took a greater effort than any battle waged.

If the arguments became more embittered and destroyed their love, he thought, Ruth could easily start anew. She was successful and attractive and still only thirty-one. She still had a few lives left; she could still have children.

He had let his last birthday pass him by—he hadn't even answered the phone. They went out to dinner together at the restaurant in the park. He was pleased with the watch she'd given him—an Omega with a white dial, a beautiful present, even though it looked, she said, a bit thin on his wrist. Later, when he'd already had a good bit to drink and had mumbled 'forty-*six*' a few times in disbelief, she said she hoped he wouldn't take it wrong, her present. It was meant to remind him of the time they had left, not the time that had already passed.

Around midnight, when she came into the room and lay down beside him, he awoke from a light sleep. They lay in the dark, listening to each other's breathing.

• • •

Friso Walta, Ruth's younger brother, is the kind of man all the Natashas of this world call 'darling'; he has the emaciated face of a visionary poet, and the manners of a man born in a three-piece suit. They run their fingers through his blond beard and caress his hair in his sleep. He once herded sheep in Australia and played music in the streets of Lima, but that life came to an end. The woman with whom he fell in love turned out be an even bigger egomaniac than he was: she left a letter behind on the table and abandoned him with their child in the projects of south-east Amsterdam.

The little boy's name is Hunter, after the American cult writer; he was conceived on a beach in Bali and born in a hospital in Honfleur. He is almost four, but can barely pronounce his father's name, because the muscles of his mouth are too feeble. On rare occasions, one can make out a word amid his babbling: 'Oop' when he has a dirty nappy, 'dwink botta' when he's thirsty. His father plays the guitar and sings 'Oh baby, baby, it's a wild world' until tears come to his eyes. The child suffers from chronic diarrhoea because the only food in the house is powdered milk. One afternoon, they take the subway to the centre of Amsterdam, and a shocked Surinamese woman says: 'That child is way too white, man! You need to put it in the sun!'

On the sidewalk along Rokin, Friso sings Cat Stevens songs. Passers-by toss coins into his hat, and he smiles meekly. His voice is high, a bit nasal. The child sleeps in its wagon.

When Hunter is five, he goes to school. The teacher reports his language deficiency to Child Welfare. In her report she writes that he has the developmental level of a three-year-old. He prefers crawling on the floor to walking, and has had no inoculations because his father feels that he has 'the right to go through the childhood illnesses'. Threatened with having the child placed in a foster home, Friso agrees to allow family and parenting support—twice a week, a woman comes by to play with the child and do language games with him; when she is around, the boy sometimes awakes from his lethargy. On Wednesday afternoons, another woman comes to teach Friso some of the rudiments of parenting. Hunter loses some of his pallor and is now able to form simple sentences such as 'Hunter wants banana', 'Daddy is dumb', and 'Here comes the seal'. The social workers report that supervision remains necessary, but that the 'father appears capable of understanding the instructions and carrying them out'. From now on, the home help will visit once every three months, which comes down to an average of only two moments of contact a year: missed appointments are not rescheduled, but simply cancelled.

So Hunter Walta grows up, a pale, unsure child, under the care of a father who adheres to a form of world-withdrawal that comes down to neglecting himself and his child.

One morning the bells rings, and Ruth opens the door. 'My beautiful sister,' the man in the doorway says. She lets him in, not knowing quite what to say. He has a child with him, hiding behind his legs. She squats down and says: 'And you, little man, you must be Hunter?'

At the kitchen table, she asks him why he's come. 'Mum gave me your address,' he says. She looks at the boy. There's something wrong with him, but she can't quite figure out what. He is sucking hard on his pacifier.

'And the gentlemen of the house,' Friso asks, 'where is he?'

'Edward works,' she says.

'That has to happen, too.' He looks around, with the look of a burglar. 'Nice house, ma'am. And a playground around the corner. Everything in readiness for a child.'

Somewhere in his youth she lost him. He has elected to be a stranger in her life, in everyone's life.

He wants to leave the child with her for a week; he needs to arrange something in Montreux, but he doesn't say what.

That evening, she tells Edward: 'He was gone before I even realised it.'

'Hit-and-run tactics.'

They look at the child asleep on the couch, beneath a quilt. His blond Walta hair hangs down over his face; he is breathing through his mouth. 'He's a cute kid,' Ruth says.

'And his mother, where is she?'

'She's French, I believe. Mum said she left Hunter with him. I could always take him up to Friesland …'

'But?'

'He's my nephew. I don't know him at all. I could take a couple of days off …'

And so they end up with a child, for a week. Edward can't stop worrying that her brother won't show up at all, that he'll leave them stuck with the child. 'Ep' is what the boy calls him. He takes him to the playground in Wilhelmina Park a few times. 'Ep, uppy-daisy!' Hunter refuses to climb the ladder on the slide on his own; Edward swings him up onto the platform, and Hunter shrieks as he slides down. In terms of motor skills, he's far behind the other, much younger children. He waggles around between the playground equipment on his fat little legs, never losing sight of Edward. Generally speaking he is withdrawn, but he occasionally throws little tantrums in which he takes shovels and spades away from other kids. The children are called Sophie or Olivier, they have learned that violence is reprehensible, and so they submit passively and with forbearance, victims of their parents' strategy. Edward silently eggs the boy on; a few moments later, he returns the toys himself.

Ruth comes over to meet them. She's wearing an orange woollen shawl — it's one of those summers that just won't show up. Above the treetops hangs a motionless grey sky: igneous rock.

She has never thought of herself as a *mother*; in fact, she is still living in a long, drawn-out girlishness, but lately, when her hands are busy and her thoughts roll around aimlessly, she sometimes sees a child in front of her. It has no face — it consists only of light, soft material, the essence of the childlike. They are daydreams, but sometimes the images crowd forward in her consciousness and become *thoughts*, their specific gravity increases. Edward sits down beside her on the bench, she sees drops of sweat along his hairline. He smiles, 'What do you think, shall we make one of these, too?', and at that moment she is so desperately in love with him that tears come to her eyes.

There is another thought inside her that barely owns up to words: with a child, her relationship with this introverted man will gain more meaning—the dynamics of *Dritte im Bunde*, the third in a chord. The prospect of being with him all her life, without someone else to disturb the peace, makes her feel trapped. They will gradually become covered in ice crystals, tiny white spangles in his beard and on her face, around her eyes and her mouth, and slowly harden into a friendly pose; in a frozen state, waiting for the end.

He throws his arm around her shoulders and pulls her into the lee of his body. Hunter looks at them, afraid of losing Edward's attention, then goes and sits alone on the seesaw.

That evening, with the boy asleep in the bed they bought for him at IKEA, she suddenly says: 'Ed, maybe I do want a child.'

He is silent for a moment, then says: 'That's what I was afraid of.'

She examines his face, but sees that he is well disposed and not cynical. She comes over and stands in front of him, kneels like a slave before her master, and slips her hand into his. 'Could I ask what else you're thinking?' she asks, half solemnly.

He gives a little nod upstairs, where Hunter is sleeping. 'Is it because of him?'

She shrugs.

'I think,' he says then, 'that we should just do it … Our lives, everything, it's all going to change, but … I mean, the whole world has children, so why can't we?' And, a little later: 'What'll we have, a boy or a girl?'

Refilling his glass, he thinks about the effect of alcohol on the quality of his sperm—about that, and the dwindling desire for sex that he's experienced lately, which he blames on drinking.

• • •

They marry in the spring of 2005, in Saint-Valery-sur-Somme. A gentle rain had fallen earlier that morning, but the clouds above the ocean have now been driven away. The chapel is in the fields above the village, and a small group of guests has assembled in the wooden pews. Of the important people, only Friso and Hunter are missing. Ruth had called her brother a few times the night before, but he hadn't answered.

'Maybe he'll just show up later on,' she says. 'Hey, hello, here I am …'

Edward lays a hand on her cheek and caresses away

the sad turn of her mouth.

The priest is an icy ascetic. He stands atop the tomb of a mediaeval hermit called Walaric, who is honoured here as Saint Valery. A holy man, miracles happen at his grave. Ceremoniously and resolutely, the priest pronounces his blessing over the marriage.

The sun is at its zenith. Grains of rice gleam in the light. 'I didn't understand a word of it, but it was lovely,' Edward's father-in-law says. They drink champagne, and walk down to the *source de la fidélité* that flows from the bottom of the hill beneath the church — a dark spring, closed off with iron grillwork. The priest has the key, but he has already climbed into his Peugeot and driven off down the narrow dirt road. Edward and Ruth pose beneath the word FIDES chiselled in the stone above the gateway, toss coins through the grillwork into the black water behind, and kiss again. Everyone cheers and claps.

Tipsy and happy, they walk through the fields back to the village. The estuary at the bottom of the hill is drained; the mud flats glisten in the sunlight.

In the mirror of the men's room in the restaurant on the quay, he glances at himself. With his beard streaked with grey and the two top buttons of his snowy-white shirt unbuttoned, he looks like a Greek singer.

On the tables are silver platters full of shellfish on ice, an image of plenty. Edward looks over at his wife, how she cracks open a crab leg and picks out the meat. Just this once, she says, because she doesn't know how to say 'sustainably caught' in French. He wishes his mother could have shared in his happiness. Almost across from him is his father, his hair white and frothy, his new girlfriend at his side. Will he ever again be as happy as he was with his mother, Edward wonders. Is a human truly, fully equipped to love only once, as he once read somewhere, or does one get another chance? Is life that generous? He admits the sweet pain of the thought of a life without her, and can't imagine that his cup would ever run so full again.

He drinks cool, light-green wine, Ruth whispers in his ear that she loves him, and that later, when they're alone—

There we leave them, in the midst of their happiness, at the mouth of the river that rises forth two hundred and fifty kilometres inland.

• • •

When Ruth just didn't get pregnant, they went in for a fertility test. Edward jerked off in a hospital room equipped with well-thumbed smut and a silent movie from the prehistory of pornography bouncing across the screen. He closed his eyes and thought about Marjolein van Unen and her breasts, her skin glistening with youth, as she popped the snaps on her lab coat, one by one. She leant back on her stool, her back against the fume cupboard, and let him go in …

The receptionist jotted down his particulars on a label, which she then stuck to the pot, so that his seed would not be taken for that of the North African who sat beside him, expressionless as a piece of fruit. A little later they passed each other again, driving at a snail's pace across the parking lot: the North African in a weathered Fiat, he in his Volkswagen Touareg. His sperm may have been as worthless as an immigrant's, but his car was a cut above.

Only 35 per cent of his cells were viable, the gynaecologist told him a few weeks later, 'more or less the percentage you'd expect from a truck driver'. The bulletin board behind the doctor's back was hung with birth announcements. Joy, joy. He told Edward about his research, which focused on exceptionally fertile men. 'If you want to find out what makes Porsches so good,' he said, 'then you need to study Porsches, not Trabants.' They left the office only after the gynaecologist had told them about the future they could expect: a route that would lead them in ascending degrees of despair past the wonders of modern assisted-reproductive technology. There was intrauterine insemination, in-vitro fertilisation, and if even that didn't work there was always ICSI — intracytoplasmic sperm injection — in which the liveliest sperm cells were fished out from among all the dead material and injected into the plasma of the egg cell. Two fertilised egg cells were then put back into the uterus, which accounted for the preponderance of twins born after this treatment. In the parking garage, she ran her index finger over his crotch and said: 'A *Trabant*, honey-pie?'

Dutifulness crept into their sex life. They made love with awkward bodies, Ruth keeping track of when they had to. Abstaining from alcohol on weekdays made him so grumpy that she would shout: 'Well then, open a bottle of wine, for Christ's sake!'

In the evening, as they stood together before the bathroom mirror, he saw a young woman and an old man. At fifty, every man has the face he deserves, Orwell had said, but Edward was convinced that that moment had already arrived on the cusp of his forty-eighth birthday. There were days when it looked as though he had never wiped the sleep from his eyes.

He and Ruth, he noted, had slid gradually into a tragic vortex of age. She had adapted to fit his years, rather than his personality. Yes, that's how it had gone: she became older because of him, and he got even older than he was because of her. When naked in front of her, he was careful not to bend down from the waist, for then his belly and breasts seemed to separate from his frame and dangle in shapeless pleats; he would squat instead to pick up the cap of the toothpaste tube. He tried not to groan aloud when he did so.

Perhaps this, he thought, was his pain, the pain the Buddha had called the principal source of suffering: the acute awareness of disintegration. With a wife his own age it would have been different, he suspected; they would have grown old together in dignity, and closed their eyes discreetly to each other's decline.

Ruth and he would not grow old together. He already *had* grown old and, if the general demographic precepts held true, he would not become old enough to see her do so. What he would have given to be able to return to the very beginning, before things like this began to torment him so. The triumph he'd felt at that evening's conquest! But now, six years later, he knew it was a victory that could never be secured. What had started as a triumph was now an unequal battle.

Each morning he took a handful of pills, the benefits of which had been proven only barely or not at all. He was vaguely ashamed of his unreasoned belief that seaweed, ginseng, and royal jelly could provide him with youth and strength, but placed this in perspective by recalling how Herman Wigboldus had asked him to wipe his feet on the patch of lawn before his house.

Otherwise he was as unlike his old mentor as he was unlike Jaap Gerson; forceful personages both, who felt that happiness was their just desert. They dropped on life like paratroopers and took it by force. God, such nonchalant power, Edward thought—power he knew he could imitate, but did not actually possess. He could seduce a woman with its intimation, but not convince her in the long run.

Ruth had been in the shower for a long time, a sign that she was getting ready to have sex with him. He wondered whether he was capable of summoning up the requisite lust. Maybe if he licked her first.

She rubbed a peephole in the steamy shower door and pressed her nose against it. He planted a kiss on it. 'I'll be there in a minute,' she said from beneath the hissing spray. He lay in bed, toying with his organ in the hope of instilling a little life into it beforehand.

He remembered well what it was like to get a hard-on just by pointing at it, as opposed to the result of focused efforts that Ruth had once described as 'hardish'.

'The only head start I have on you,' he once told his students, 'is that I know what it's like to be you, while you haven't the faintest idea what it's like to be me. That's our only advantage, otherwise the world is furnished to accommodate you people. We may hold the buying power, but you possess the far more valuable capital of the future, whatever that may turn out to be.'

When Ruth slid in beside him a little later and whispered 'Sorry, love, you're on duty again', he cursed the fact, and not for the first time, that one could grow accustomed to a beauty even as exceptional as hers. Everything became humdrum, and what was habituation if not death's gate? Her beauty didn't lead inevitably to randiness; on the contrary, someone like Marjolein van Unen excited him with undeniably more urgency than his own wife, who was a thousand times prettier. And with that girl in mind—the finger he slid up her butthole—he was able to live up to his obligations.

• • •

Socio-psychological research at the University of Nijmegen showed that the chance of a male being unfaithful during his wife's pregnancy was twenty-seven times greater than at any other point in a marriage. A man contained himself as well as he could during his wife's periods of illness and recovery—and, more generally, during the slow but certain process of the loss of beauty and vitality—but during her pregnancy he went all-out. The periodic sexual obsession of his bloated wife frightened him, her protruding labia and excessively slimy cunt made him a bit nauseous. In addition, he experienced the clear and generally quite correct premonition that after the child was born his life would be more or less over—all the reason one needed to commit adultery.

After a departmental sightseeing tour by boat of Amsterdam's canals and the River IJ, followed by drinks at Hoppe's on the Spui, Edward decided not to take the night train back to Utrecht, but to go by taxi. Beside him in the back seat was Marjolein van Unen. As they kissed, she opened his zipper and jerked him off until he almost came. He had enough self-control to push her hand away in time. They had the cabby drop them at the central station and found a public toilet. Fishing a one-euro coin from his pocket, he thought: a euro to take a piss is fairly steep, but a euro for a fuck is a real bargain. He locked the door behind them and pulled off her trousers and panties. She sat down on the toilet bowl and leaned back, her hands resting on the lid; he unbuckled his trousers and knelt between her legs. That was how he fucked Marjolein van Unen for the first time, beneath the glow of purplish fluorescent tubes and amid the odour of stale piss. He came as though it was the very first time, and in a sense it was. She leaned against the back wall with a saintly smile. So this was it, he thought, this is what it was all about, this border-crossing from which there was no return—the cunt of Marjolein van Unen, the centre of the universe.

Ruth's pregnancy went serenely, dreamily; she was bothered almost not at all by the discomforts her girlfriends talked about, the chronic nausea and inexplicable pains. She felt a bit distracted, but in a way that pleased her, as though she was barely in contact with the physical world. She converted her study into a nursery, and went in there every day for a while to rearrange the little rompers, socks, and caps, her movements charged with a glow of expectation for which she had no words. She told no one that it was going to be a boy, and that his name would be Morris. Even before the child was born, Edward already knew what it was to be part of the little conspiracy against the outside world that a family is. Not only Ruth was pregnant, but the whole house was—it radiated out into the park and far beyond. Their principal conversations were reduced to friendly chitchat about who their son would be and which traits they hoped to recognise in him and which not. Life compacted to a cocoon with room only for them. In the morning she remained behind in it, and he left for the institute, where there awaited the encounter with Marjolein van Unen. She proved a discreet mistress, but still he had the daily sensation of being transported light years away from the padded little world he had just left. He had locked himself out, and struggled against the thought that this was irreversible.

She was twenty-eight, the age Ruth had been when he'd met her. She had a two-room flat in the Kanaaleiland district; he asked her to put away the scented candles, for Ruth's pregnancy had whetted her sense of smell.

'The things I do for you,' she said.

'I'm your boss.'

'Come on then, boss.'

She was small and slim and limber, and possessed the hunger of thin women. She knew how to move her pelvis independently of the rest of her body, and was what the Emperor Tiberius had termed a 'sphincter artist' in the sense that, straddling him and seemingly immobile, she could make him come by means of powerful internal contractions. She did her best—she had taken courses in Tantra, and applied the techniques she'd learned with a barely perceptible smile. He didn't know exactly what she wanted from him. 'What does your boyfriend think of all this?' he asked once. She raised a finger to her lips. 'Sssh. Everything you say out loud comes back to you.'

Her cunt was well proportioned and hairless, and she knew no shame. Sometimes, on her hands and knees in front of him, she would shake her hair out of her eyes, and it took a while before he understood what he was seeing. *She acts as though there's a camera running* ... the vain endowment of pornography.

'Have you got anything to drink?' he asked, and a few moments later she came into the room with a bottle of Metaxa she'd brought home from Greece. They lay back on the pillows; he held the glass in one hand and put the other between her legs, where it was open and wet. 'I already knew everything,' he said. 'The way you taste, how you feel, smell, I knew it all already.'

'How boring then,' she said.

'On the contrary.'

'Did you get a hard-on when you thought about me?'

'A thousand times over,' he said.

She was from Veghel; her father had died when she was seven. A month later, there was a new man in the house. 'My mother couldn't stand being alone. She still can't.'

When she was twelve, the man had assaulted her; she kept silent, but left home when she was only fifteen. She said those were 'difficult times', but meanwhile she had finished high school on her own and was admitted to the lab technicians' school in Leeuwarden, as far as possible from her parental home.

'What year were you born in?' she asked.

'Fifty-eight,' he said.

Without a hint of surprise, she said: 'Just like my mother. Which month?'

'May.'

'That's funny. Then you're older than she is … A Taurus, I bet.'

The hard light of a late afternoon at the end of summer. The merciless hour. Moroccan boys raced up and down the street on mopeds. With a tender gesture, she smoothed back a few of the long hairs protruding from his eyebrows.

He saw framed photographs of her with a well-built young man. In one of them, he was wearing a wetsuit; in the other, which showed them embracing in some departure hall, a Dutch Marine Corps uniform. 'He's stationed in Afghanistan,' she said. 'We Skype almost every day.'

'When he comes back,' Edward said, 'he'll be a veteran. Thirty-something, and already —'

'He's thirty-two.'

His name was Michel; he had taken care of her when she was in a bad way. 'Without him, I wouldn't be here. Not like this.'

Hanging across from the toilet was a poster with the text: 'If nothing ever changed, there would be no butterflies.' When she massaged his feet, he began to weep. No one had ever touched his neglected feet like this.

'A lot of meridians come together in your feet,' she said. And: 'If you ask me, you're a lot more sensitive than you think.'

When he came home, he didn't know whether he was Zhuangzi dreaming that he was a butterfly, or a butterfly dreaming that he was Zhuangzi. But at night in Wilhelmina Park across the way there crept a man with an automatic rifle, and camouflage stripes on his face, who forced his way into the house and opened fire on the double bed and the crib beside it.

• • •

He dreams about it for the first time during her pregnancy: how she leaves him and takes their child with her. He won't get them back. He can go on living in Utrecht or move to Amsterdam, and there is also a variation in which he returns to his childhood village. It makes no difference; he has been cut loose from everything. He can turn left or right, there is nothing to keep him from going in any direction whatsoever—only the way back, that has been cut off. Somewhere in the whitened world, he stands, frozen, catatonic. He tries to pick up his life the way it was before he met her, but he has truly become too old for that. He will remain alone and, disappointed and filled with loathing, occasionally meet someone through a dating site, and sometimes he will burst into tears at his memories. This is what he's made of his life, a barrens stretching out on all sides. Of all the feelings he's ever had, only fear and confusion remain. Register this man as childless, a man who has known no happiness all his days …

The dream contained elements that were outspokenly practical, he felt, and did not seem to belong in the dead, empty space in which he moved. Whatever the case, he awoke each time in the bed he shared with Ruth with such an overwhelming sense of relief that he swore right then and there to better his ways. With a shiver of loneliness he crept up against her pregnant, sleeping body.

He had made a mess of it, but things could still be set aright, it wasn't too late. She never needed to know about it and, if he only stopped doing all the things that were dragging him down, if he tied the loose ends together, he would forget about it, too, in time. It would have never happened, or it would become like the memory of a book you'd read as a child, where you could still summon up the general mood, but where the events themselves had dissolved into thin air.

• • •

One early morning in January, Ruth woke him and said calmly: 'I think the contractions have started.' At six-thirty they left the house, the bag he carried containing baby clothes and diapers and her nightgown. The road was quiet. His hand rested on her thigh. The sky was cloudless, heralding a clear, cold day. Frost glistened on the grass along the shoulder. 'I thought it was just a stomach-ache,' she said, 'but when I started counting, it was so regular ...'

Only two of the rooms in the delivery ward were occupied. They rubbed gel on her belly and strapped on a heart-rate monitor. The obstetrician briefed her again about the lumbar puncture, which she could ask for at any time. Ruth grimaced under the force of a contraction. 'Try to relax,' the woman said.

Edward had gone along a few times to the haptonomist; he had learned how to reassure her and how they could breathe together, but, now that the time had come, he knew that the only thing required of him was his unobtrusive presence.

'Will you stay with me?' she asked.

He ran his hand over her sweaty forehead. 'I'm right here. Don't worry.'

Half an hour later, she was on all fours on the bed and bellowing; the pain had thrown her back into an animal state. Vaguely embarrassed, he thought of the shrieks of the pigs she had heard as a young girl.

'*Don't. Put. Your. Hand. There!*' she moaned between two contractions. He quickly pulled it away from the small of her back.

'It's going wonderfully, sweetheart,' the female obstetrician said. 'You're doing a great job.'

On occasion, the woman would leave the room and not come back for half an hour. Edward stood a little distance from the bed and looked at his wife. It was something that had to be borne alone, the pain itself remained hidden. He saw only the outward manifestations of it—the screaming, the undulating melodies of suffering.

Empathy was the key to the pain of others, Ruth had said once. Troubled, he plumbed his inner self. There was his wife. She was suffering. The pain, they said, was like that of an amputation with no anaesthetic. The distortion in her voice made him shiver. He would have comforted her if she could have stood his touch, but he couldn't get through to her suffering. There she was and here he was, powerless and useless. He couldn't cross the line. Almost everyone in her world seemed able to do that —she and her friends were fundamentally united with the world's suffering, as divided into subsections like the repression of women, political prisoners, animals used for food, vivisection, and Tibetans. Their suffering impacted them directly, emotionally; their nervous systems were intertwined with those of others. The other person's pain was a precondition for a meaningful life.

A second obstetrician had come into the room now. The number of manoeuvres and the nervous urgency increased. 'Spinal puncture!' Ruth said. 'I want it!'

The obstetrician soothed her. 'It won't take long now. You're almost at complete dilation.'

'Now!'

'You can start pressing in just a little bit—hang in there.'

The screaming faded into a quiet moaning. A life-and-death struggle. When an Aztec woman died during childbirth, she was buried with military honours.

'Sweetheart,' Edward said insistently, 'he's almost there. Can you hold out a little?'

'Fuckfuckfuck.'

She lashed out at him when he came too close to the foot of the bed—she didn't want him to see what was happening there. From between her legs, the obstetrician looked up at him and nodded. 'And … push!' she said. 'Push!'

When the child came out, it was as though the obstetrician was trying to catch a wet bar of soap. In a single movement, she laid the child on Ruth's stomach. 'My little man,' Ruth said, laughing and weeping at the same time, 'there you are, finally.'

Edward kissed her fevered forehead and leaned down over his son, a bluish little creature covered in blood and mucus. He smelled strongly of iron. So this was it, he thought, this triumph. He was grinning from ear to ear. The obstetrician handed him a pair of scissors, and he cut the tough, rubbery umbilical. Morris was bathed and weighed, and when they went home hours later with the child in the carrier, they felt as frightened and indomitable as a teenage couple in a stolen car.

• • •

The first days with a newborn child: happiness as delicate as gold wire. The memories can't be held onto; the euphoria comes in quick, successive waves. There is a photo of Edward, lying on the couch with his eyes closed and his mouth open slightly. One arm is tucked behind his head; with the other, he holds Morris, who is sleeping on his chest. A photo from that same series is used for the birth announcement: it shows only the boy, his skull covered with fine, blond hair, and his lips twisted in a cramp that could pass for a smile.

It is as though the atmosphere of benevolent household happiness has been made flesh, Edward thinks, as though he could grab hold of it if he wanted to. There are almost no thoughts of the life outside. He longs for nothing but this. He doesn't want to think about Marjolein. It makes him restless. The ante has been upped. There is everything to lose.

When they ran into each other on the institute parking lot and spoke for a few minutes, she had said she'd already noticed that something had changed. She understood, she said: after all, it *was* truly something, what he was going through now. Little clouds came out of her mouth. She waved to him from the car; he smiled gratefully. This was the end to his faux pas, he thought. It had come easier than he'd expected.

• • •

A few months after Morris is born, Ruth pronounces the term 'fussy baby', but then in the form of a denial. 'He's not a fussy baby,' she says. 'He's just having trouble making a landing on Earth.' The image of his son as a space traveller appeals to Edward. Knocked out of orbit and stranded in the wrong galaxy — but then where *does* he belong?

Morris, it seems, can be lulled to sleep only by means both subtle and prolonged, and just when they think they've found such a routine, it starts all over again.

It began two weeks after he was born, as though he was tormented by pain or by having left behind his life as a space traveller. He rips their nights apart with crying. The cradle is on her side of the bed; she sleeps with one hand on his stomach, and when she tries to withdraw it, he awakes with a start and cries. They spend the nights wandering, the baby on one arm, rocking and hushing him. The serene happiness of the first weeks has made way for irritability and despair. Morris is given Zantac against reflux, and Edward is too exhausted to make a smart remark about its manufacturer: GlaxoSmithKline.

This, therefore, is how noise enters Edward's life — like a cordon of striking truckers leaning on their horns, preceded by a parade by the Association of Muffler-Free Scooters. A hundredfold Semitic widows in disarray bring up the rear. There is no way he can protect himself; it worms its way into his defenceless ears, and crawls under his skin. The passing noises of the world, too, reduce him to a shambles — a magpie perched on the gutter, a scream from the park, anything at all can drag his son up from his hard-won sleep. In the frequencies emitted by cats meowing in the garden, or planes high in the sky, Edward hears the sound of Morris crying; his heart starts pounding, the hair on the back of his neck stands up. *He's awake ... Goddamn it, he's awake again ...*

At the institute, he sometimes looks up in fright from his monitor, hearing his son's cry in the shriek of a dry hinge.

'He's not crying for the fun of it,' Ruth says, 'or just to vex you. You seem to forget that something is really bothering him.'

The baby boy's pain has welled up from the depths of his vital organs to his brain, yet the cause itself remains invisible. Neither Zantac nor Motilium seem to help. Ruth packs him off to doctors and herbal therapists; an osteopath slides his practised hands gently up and down the baby's locomotor apparatus. They hang a hairdryer in his cradle, because the sound seems to soothe him.

By the time a baby is six months old, Ruth and Edward tell each other, the worst of it is usually over. Even the most persistent of fussy babies calms down then. Six months, in any case, is a point far beyond their endurance. They will never make it to August; the crying would have torn them to the ground long before that, just as the walls of Jericho crumbled beneath the persistent roar of the rams' horns.

Her patience is greater than his; she never has the urge to silence Morris by force. She is surprised by the flames of impotent rage that flare up in Edward, and takes over when she feels he is rocking the baby 'unnaturally'. 'He'll never quiet down that way,' she says.

His son, the organ pipe.

Sometimes, when Morris seems to recognise him, Edward is touched. His little red hands clutch at nothingness. Edward caresses his thin blond hair, his face smoother than smooth. At the fontanel, you can see the beating of the blood.

• • •

The days are long and hot, unseasonably early that year. In the kitchen, flies swarm around the cat box and the cutting board. He swats them with a rolled-up dishtowel. Each time he thinks he's killed them all, new ones appear. They burst open under the dry whacks of the towel, but don't always die right away. In the block of sunlight on the floor, he watches their death throes. They pull wet tracks behind them across the tiles, an alphabet of fly pain.

In 1780, Jeremy Bentham wrote:

The day has been, I grieve it to say in many places it is not yet past, in which the greater part of the species, under the denomination of slaves, have been treated ... upon the same footing as ... animals are still. The day may come, when the rest of the animal creation may acquire those rights which never could have been withholden from them but by the hand of tyranny. The French have already discovered that the blackness of skin is no reason why a human being should be abandoned without redress to the caprice of a tormentor. It may come one day to be recognised, that the number of legs, the villosity of the skin, or the termination of the *os sacrum*, are reasons equally insufficient for abandoning a sensitive being to the same fate. What else is it that should trace the insuperable line? Is it the faculty of reason, or perhaps, the faculty for discourse? ... the question is not, Can they reason? nor, Can they talk? but, Can they suffer?

The page was stuck to the bulletin board in the bathroom. It was *ammunition*. Long ago he had made the mistake of telling Ruth about his animal testing lines. The course of viral infections was easiest to see in ferrets. It was precision work; with a few slight mutations, a deadly influenza virus could change into a mild variation, while mild viruses could suddenly become deadly.

Sometimes he looked through Ruth's eyes at the animals in their cages and saw that boredom was the first form of suffering to which they were exposed.

They no longer groomed themselves, and they exhibited compulsive behaviour. Endorphins provided some relief from their stimulus-starved existence. The longer and more often he watched, the weaker his denial of their suffering became. It was because of the shattered nights, he thought. His son's crying had debilitated him. The ideas of his wife and of a British utilitarian had broken like parasites through his faltering defences. He had even become more susceptible to certain TV programs. While watching one program in which old sweethearts were reunited, he had to fight back the tears.

Long ago he had been taught that animals knew no pain—an old Cartesian tenet that had been revised only recently. The denial had become more sophisticated these days. Animals could experience pain, but not suffering. Suffering was reserved for humans. People owed their suffering to their consciousness. To be more precise: pain augmented by the memory of pain and the expectation of pain to come was one of the causes of human suffering. Animals possessed no such consciousness, and if they actually felt pain, it disappeared as soon as the pain stimulus was taken away. As his son was still largely non-conscious, Edward assumed that he did not suffer, but that he *did* feel pain.

It was a mechanistic approach that worked well as long as you didn't muddy it up with tricky questions and the notion of interspecific empathy, which—until recently—he had dismissed as sentimental. It was hard enough already to feel for the pain of one's own species, Edward thought, so more or less impossible to understand the pain of other animals.

Ferrets who had experienced the hypodermic shied away, trembling, from the white-gloved hand; they panted in fear. Edward, now that he was perched on a stool before the cages and trying to *enter into* that, was tempted to interpret this as memory. It was reflexive behaviour, prompted by nociceptive neurons in the spinal cord and not by the brain, but it was still the result of negative experiences. If this was a primitive form of *physical memory*, couldn't one also speak of a primitive form of suffering? The physiology of the mammals in the lab did not differ essentially from that of humans—the similarity was precisely why they were used. And, just like people, they were ruled by pain and pleasure. It was less complex, but the same principle.

The consequence of Bentham's reasoning, he thought, would have to be a new categorical system, a taxonomy of suffering. A new Linnaeus would have to arise to classify the pain. There was still no instrument that could objectively measure it. To rate pains in humans, a scale from 1 to 10 was used, whereby the patients themselves could report on the intensity. But there was as yet no instrument like a thermometer to read off the pain in tissues and organs. In order to arrive at a new system like that, Edward thought, one would first have to be able to measure pain. The pain stimulus might be objective (the pulling-out of a fingernail, or the poking-out of an eye), but the experience of that stimulus was personal. And how could you measure these things in creatures who could not express themselves verbally: in a horse, a dog, in Morris?

In his daydream, pain is accorded the same kind of fanaticism they applied to AIDS in his day. Laboratories work overtime; instruments gleam in the cold light. The mammalian nociceptive chain is poked at with sophisticated tools, the network of nerve endings, fibres, and ganglia laid bare—somewhere in that chain must lie the secret. The tortures become increasingly refined; needle-thin pointers give scores to the umpteenth decimal point. To what extent do animals experience pain? Do they remember pain, and fear new pain? Can they *suffer* ...?

The world waits in anticipation of the new taxonomy from the pain factories. If the suffering of other species corresponds to or is even equal to the measure in which humans suffer, the consequences will be inestimable. The anthropocentric view that places man at the centre of the kingdom of pain will become obsolete, and the torture of billions of test and farm animals will be seen as mankind's greatest disgrace. When animals are given the *right to suffer*, there will be no end to the *mea culpas*, the apologies, the commemorative centres and monuments of remorse.

All sounds from the laboratories are broadcast on a radio frequency allotted specially to that purpose. The pain of vertebrates; the pain of invertebrates. Some animals writhe and shudder, but cannot make themselves understood. (The radio falls silent.) Other animals roar, screech, whistle, peep, hiss, and sigh—all fairly clear graduators of pain, but most of them hard to interpret. Radio Pain is on the air around the clock; we listen to their cries in the darkness.

The *Bhagavad Gita* defines man as a wound with nine openings. The great pain project defines the whole world as a gaping wound, its openings innumerable.

Edward rubbed his eyes. He was so tired.

• • •

In late May, Edward takes part in a four-hour live radio program organised by the VPRO, one of the major Dutch broadcast organisations. It involves the simulation of an outbreak of H5N1; a crisis team has been assembled to take the requisite measures. Jaap Gerson is the team leader; the others include a police chief, a senior official from the Ministry of Internal Affairs, and a retired general from Wassenaar. Edward has been invited as director of the Laboratory for Zoonoses and Environmental

Microbiology, and as advisor to the WHO. Hundreds of fatalities have already been reported in Asia and Southern Europe. In the Netherlands, the number of infections is spreading rapidly.

During the marathon broadcast, reporters—supposedly on the scene—keep feeding the players new facts and situations. 'Millions of people may succumb to this invasion,' the moderator says in his introduction, 'but unlike in *The War of the Worlds*, there is now no bacteria to save us; no, it is precisely a virus that threatens all mankind.'

A flight from Bangkok, headed for Amsterdam, is now somewhere over Turkey. All of the passengers and crew are probably infected. The retired general says that the army will provide assistance at the airport. 'Everyone on that plane will be placed in quarantine,' he says. 'An unpleasant but necessary measure.' The general has left his villa in Wassenaar to have a good time at the studio. One of the program's female researchers keeps his glass of white wine filled. Edward watches him so closely—how he signals to the girl, points at his glass, and mimes the word 'ice!'—that he sometimes loses track of the conversation. He himself is drinking beer; it's hot in the studio.

Gerson explains what is going on in the laboratories. 'What we're waiting for is the development of a virus inhibitor. Then we'll have to produce a few million doses, so the whole thing could take a while.'

A reporter announces that hundreds of passengers at Schiphol Airport are refusing to submit to forced isolation. Groups of men are attempting to break out.

'But what about their luggage?' Edward says. No one laughs.

Many of the passengers are ill. Fighting has broken out. In the hospitals, too, people are refusing to be confined.

'And well they might,' Edward says. He explains the meaning of Ro, the basic reproduction number, the measure of the virus's reach. Within ten days, millions of people can become infected.

'So?'

'During the outbreak of hog cholera, we culled ten million pigs; during the foot-and-mouth crisis, more than a hundred thousand. Neither of those diseases is dangerous to humans, but H7N7—which appeared in 2003—was. Thirty-five million chickens had to be disposed of during that outbreak. So what I'm talking about now is requisite measures: you have to have the guts to take them. An ethicist might say that you're not allowed to take even one life in order to save hundreds of others, but we're here to make decisions, aren't we?'

The moderator repeats the figure, thirty-five million. His dumbfoundedness is real.

'Gassed, all of them,' Edward said. 'I think … you

have to dare to take unpopular measures in order to keep worse from happening.'

'Are you saying … gas *people*?' the moderator says.

Edward has his hands on the table in front of him, straddling the mike. 'They're incurably ill. Sources of infection.'

A silence descends.

'I mean —' He realises his mistake; the unguarded moment. The blood rushes to his head. He recalls the stories about Gerson's parental home in Hilversum, close to the studio, where the blinds are always closed. Jaap grew up in a blacked-out house. *Sperrzeit*, around the clock. Light was life, light was joy. On the Polish plain, the light had been extinguished.

'The words "unpleasant" and "necessary" have been mentioned a few times already …' The moderator tries to get things going again.

The heat in his armpits, in his crotch, is unbearable. He is sweating. At the edge of the abyss, the discussion resumes. There are more than two hours left to go.

When he comes home, Ruth says: 'Christ, Ed, had you been drinking or something?'

• • •

He was drawn to her, like water to the lowest point. He let himself go, finally; he wasn't a man made for digging in his heels. Her young skin on his, the ecstasy—he approached happiness for the first time, this was as close as he could get. She reminded him of a cat one saw slipping out of the headlights into the tall grass along the road. He felt good with her. He understood why. He could explain it; it was glorious in its simplicity. It was about the fault in the fabric of his existence, of his marriage. The ongoing affront that was his age. The creaking and the cracking of his knees. The grooves that appeared in his face without warning, and how even his brain was *slipping*. The taint of old age. That was how he understood his marriage, as a tragic lack of balance. One that could not be fixed. Not by them. For that, a third person was needed. A child, this girl. To forge a triangle. That restored the balance. It levelled the scales. It worked. For now.

He awoke with a start—their feet were lying in sunlight. *Goddamn it, oh shit.* He pulled on his clothes. 'Your T-shirt's on backwards,' she said. Her legs were spread obscenely on the sheet. Details could be one's downfall.

'We've got a problem,' Ruth said at dinner. He kept the fright under his skin. She had not noticed a thing. Since Morris had arrived, she barely seemed to see him. They slid past each other, supple as young joints.

It was about her brother, Friso. He had been evicted.

'And what are you supposed to do about that?' Edward said.

'That's what I was just about to tell you, if you'll let me.'

The story was fairly complicated, like so many from the seamy side of life. Friso was about to be relieved of his parental authority—he'd received a summons from the juvenile-court magistrate. Child Welfare had given him one last chance, which would be blown if they found out that the housing association had kicked him out of his apartment.

'Where is he now?' Edward asked.

A sound came from the baby intercom—they froze. They looked at each other, but the thing remained silent.

'He's gone with Hunter to a friend's house,' Ruth said quietly, as though Morris might hear them right through the ceiling. 'He's an alcoholic, so they can't stay there. Friso can get a new place, he says, but not until September.' She looked around the room. 'Here ... it wouldn't be possible. Not with Morris, I mean, and with you ...'

'With me?'

Again that vague smile, like a hunger striker's, as though she had taken leave of the things of the world. 'He doesn't have any money,' she said. 'Not a penny. It wouldn't be right if we didn't help him.'

'Why? Hunter might actually be better off somewhere else.'

'He's so attached to Friso, and Friso to him. He's already lost his mother. If he lost his father, too … Friso is a stable factor, despite all his mucking around.'

Edward figured it would be difficult to find a rental on such short notice, especially since it was only for a couple of months. What about a campground, he asked? It was the season for that—they could view it as a long vacation.

Ruth hesitated. Maybe there were cottages you could rent, she suggested; some campgrounds had those.

Chalets, the girl at the reception desk of the campground close to the highway told him the next morning—they rented chalets for seventy-two euros and fifty cents a night. His lips moved in silent repetition of the sum.

'It's the high season,' the girl said.

'It's the end of May,' Edward said.

She shrugged and turned back to her mobile phone.

'Ma'am?'

She looked up.

'And what if it was for three months?'

'Then you'd have to talk to Mr. Wildschut about that.'

Taped to the window were sheets of paper with the campground rules on them. They spoke of bitter intolerance. Leaving the office, he crossed the campground in search of the manager. A few pop-up tents had been set up here and there. He found the manager scolding a group of tourists who had made a mess around theirs. *Czechs*, he thought, judging from the flag sewed to one of the backpacks on the ground. The manager was wearing shorts; he had authoritarian calves — the calves of a drill sergeant. He raged on in a mixture of English and German, the Czechs staring up at him in fear. Maybe he reminded them of what their parents had told them about the terrors of the regime.

'Eastern Europeans,' he said to Edward a little later. 'They rub their shit on the walls, those people. They're swine, that's what they are.'

Untermenschen. He means Untermenschen, Edward thought. It was clear to him that he was dealing with a Nazi here, a camping-Nazi behind barbed wire and a barrier gate. He explained why he'd come.

'And who are these gentlemen you're talking about, if I may ask?'

'My nephew and his father, my brother-in-law.'

'Between houses, you say.'

It was unpleasant to have to talk to him about such things. The man led him to the chalets. Stopping in front of them, he planted his feet widely. What they were looking at were four wooden garden houses, set a little ways apart. Edward walked up and looked into one of them. Along the walls were two sets of bunk beds, with a narrow pathway between.

'Seventy-two fifty, for this?' Edward asked.

'Plus tourist tax.'

'How much is that?'

'Four times one-thirty-five a night.'

'But there are only two people.'

'Four beds, so you pay for four people. Otherwise I get into trouble with the tax department.'

Laughing a bit dazedly, Edward said: 'So three months comes down to ...'

'Six and a half thousand euros. Plus tourist tax.'

Edward looked up at the crowns of the poplars rustling in the wind. The trees marked the border of the campground. 'The houses are standing empty,' he said after a while.

'They won't be for long.' From the phone holster on his belt came the sound of an electronic *Radetzky March*. He took the call, and after a few seconds he said: 'I'll be right there.' He stuck the phone back in its holster. 'Is there anything else I can do for you?'

'I'll take it, for half that,' Edward said. 'As far as I can see, no one's staying in them, and something is always better than nothing, you've got to figure that.'

'Five thousand,' the manager said.

In the end, they agreed on four thousand euros, plus tourist tax.

Goddamned Utrecht, Edward thought a little later as he turned into the underpass beneath the highway. He felt he had been screwed, but at the same time he was willing to agree to anything in order not to have Friso and Hunter in the house. A malignant mycelium, black as ink, stretched out across time and space, connecting the campground manager and the former Dutch National Socialist Movement headquarters on Utrecht's Maliebaan, where the *Sicherheitsdienst* and SS had once been housed. Utrecht was a breeding ground for men like that. Edward's working day had yet to begin, but he felt exhausted already.

After work, he drove to Amsterdam to pick up Hunter and his father from an address on the south-east side of town. The house stank of rotting garbage and overflowing ashtrays; father and son had been sleeping on bare mattresses. They loaded three big shopping bags and a guitar into the car. 'What about the rest?' Edward asked. Friso grinned. 'It's all still inside. Sealed and repossessed, right? I can't even get into my own house.'

He owed six months' back rent; the gas and electricity had been cut off that winter. Hunter sat in the backseat and looked out at the landscape of grass and utility masts along the road. He scratched a flaky red ring on his chin. Edward felt sorry for him. 'There are lots of other kids at the campground,' he said over his shoulder. 'And there's a playground.'

The boy's smile looked like Ruth's. In the mirror,

Edward saw that a little blood vessel had burst in the corner of his right eye.

'Well, well,' Friso said as he looked around the garden house.

'It was the best we could get on such short notice,' Edward said irritatedly. 'Have you got any money?'

'No, man, nothing. They're holding back my welfare checks, too, y'understand?'

Edward gave him two hundred euros.

'You know where there's a supermarket?' Friso asked.

The campground had a store, Edward told him. But later, when they saw how expensive it was, he drove the two of them to a bigger one in the city. Darkness was already falling by the time they got back to the chalet with bags full of groceries. The next day, Edward said, he would come by with a butane-gas stove and some kitchen utensils. 'And chairs,' Friso said. 'And a table would make things easier, too.' Hunter sat reading a *Donald Duck* in the dying light.

• • •

The next evening, Edward came to the campground with Ruth and Morris. She had baked a quiche. Hunter couldn't keep his eyes off Morris. Once he had a new place, Friso said in reply to their questions, no one could put a thing on him. He would go into a program of debt restructuring, a precondition to getting his welfare payments rolling again. A new school had been found for Hunter. Ruth draped a shawl over her shoulders. 'Don't pet him so hard, Hunter,' she said, 'he's still so little.' When Edward went to take Morris over from her, she shook her head and said that he had just calmed down.

Edward wanted to go home, her brother disgusted him; a shitheel like that could never assume responsibility for a child. He would tell her later that evening, but first they sat outside in the twilight and listened as Friso, legs crossed, played a song on the little porch at the front of the cottage. Something by Leonard Cohen, Edward thought. It must have been a big hit for him around the campfire on some Asian beach. The girls probably thought he was *sensitive*, and gave themselves to him easily. It pleased Edward to think that an existence like that could end on a campground beside the A27 motorway, like Job among the ashes. All he was lacking was a certain … yes, humility. The look in those cold, goatish eyes of his was always so unmoved.

The song was over. 'That was quite lovely,' Friso said. He raised his plastic cup of wine. 'Despise the man of means, but drain his glasses.' Edward could not help feeling that he was the man of means whose glass was being drained by this freeloader.

That evening, as he was about to get into bed, Ruth said: 'Sweetheart, maybe it's not so cozy, but I think it would be better if you went upstairs. It seems to me that Morris gets very restless around you. I think it would be nicer for him if you slept upstairs.'

Her voice was friendly and calm; she said it in a very *teacherly* way. He walked out of the room without replying, angry and abashed, banished from his own bed by wife and son. Downstairs in the living room he watched TV and drank red wine, and only climbed the stairs to the loft after midnight. He dreamed of a space where people and things fell from the air, very slowly, like objects in an emulsion. When they touched the earth's surface, they sank into the ground without leaving a crack or a mark. In the midst of that slow rain of lawnmowers, upended trees, desk chairs, and people he didn't know, there stood he.

By the time he came downstairs, Ruth had already left with Morris for the day-care centre. He ate a slice of bread and drank straight out of a package of fruit juice. On the table was a note. *Message from Friso. Could you bring him a dishpan and brush too? (Don't be angry.) Love.*

The dawning day made it feel as though he had never exited his dream. Something seemed to have started, he thought, that could no longer be reversed. It had been traipsing along with him the whole time, behind him, like a shadow—but now that the sun had changed position, it was catching up with him, dark and heavy; the final alignment would be fatal.

He was waiting for the phone to ring, for a message to come in; he had a feeling of doom. But it remained still. The day passed. Nothing happened.

When he called her from the car, Ruth didn't answer. He left a message saying that he was going to buy a dishpan and brush, drop it off, and then come home. Would they have dinner together?

He sounded like a supplicant, he thought after he'd hung up. She would hear the entreaty in his voice, and despise him for it.

The campground manager had ordered Friso to clean up the mess around the chalet; someone had booked one of the other houses. 'Oh man,' Friso said, 'I sure hope it'll be a couple of sweet Eastern European babes.'

It must have been an interesting confrontation, Edward thought as he was driving home, between the Teutonic orderliness of the campground manager and Friso's fundamental indifference. Secretly, he admired him for that. Friso let himself fall over backwards, and didn't seem to care whether or not anyone caught him. Someone always did. He was the youngest child, the last of the litter, and he counted on other people to repair his mistakes for him. His character defects were never held too much against him; even Ruth still consistently came to his defence.

Edward's admiration was indistinguishable from envy. No one would ever catch *him* if he fell.

He came into the house lugging a bag full of Friso and Hunter's dirty laundry. Ruth had assumed wordlessly that he would be the house steward. She was sitting on the patio, her legs tucked up beneath her, the baby intercom on the table in front of her. 'Hey there,' she said. Motherhood had lent her something full and radiant that was not depleted by her fatigue. He leaned down. Her kiss was like the movement of one head pushing away the other.

He didn't know where to start, afraid of things he didn't want to hear. Truth was the privilege of the strong.

Ruth talked about Morris's day at the crèche; the subject served as a divider strip for them both. The garden was coming into blossom; he had planted some new clematis, with potshards piled up around their sensitive roots. The flowers they gave were purple and pink.

Ruth looked at him. 'You know, Edward, we've tried so many things …'

He forced himself to look at her.

'Nothing helps,' she said, 'not really. I'm right about that, aren't I? I stopped giving him that garbage—the Infacol and Zantac, Dophilus, all that stuff—a few weeks ago.' She shook her head. 'You never even noticed the difference.'

His face clouded over.

'I thought you wouldn't approve,' she said. 'That's why I didn't tell you. Because you —'

'You didn't ask the doctor about it, about whether you could do that, just stop with everything?' he asked.

'You know what?' she said. 'I've discovered something. Something else. I'm sure you'll think it's completely unscientific, but … sometimes a mother knows more than all the clinical studies put together.'

A sprinkler spun in the neighbours' garden, ticking as it went, every so often the water drumming against the top of a parasol.

'It's mostly in the evenings when he cries, Edward — the evenings and weekends—when he's wide awake, restless, crying. When I'm alone with him during the day, he's much calmer. The girls at the day-care say so, too.' She pulled her legs up under her again. 'During the day he does just fine, or at least a lot better. It's only in the evening. And during the weekend. I've kept track of it; it's not a coincidence. You know what it is, Edward … I'm really sorry to have to say it … but it's you.'

He waited until the rain stopped beating on the parasol, and then said: 'What's me?'

She sank back in her chair. 'The reason for his crying,' she said.

Twice he started to say something, but the words remained stuck. Ships sank in the silence between them.

'Ah-ha,' he said after a bit, as though to see whether his voice still worked.

'When you're around, he cries. It's too much of a coincidence.'

'It's insane,' he said slowly.

'I see what I see.'

'A face in the clouds, that's what you see. You can't think that way; you take him off his medicines, and then you think you can see the cause of his complaints. A chance observation with a worthless conclusion, that's what it is. And besides, *why* can't he stand having me around?'

'I don't know,' she said.

'Come on, you've thought about it, you must have.'

She looked at him, motionless as a fish. 'If you really want to know,' she said then.

They waited. Hissing, the water went round and round. Seven seconds, that's how long it took. She said: 'I think he senses that you didn't want him.'

There were some words that could not be undone. After they had sounded and dissolved into air, everything had changed; you looked back in amazement at how it used to be.

His chin dropped to his chest, as though his head had grown too heavy and broken free of his spine. He remained sitting there like that for a while. Then he straightened up and said: 'I was hoping it would turn out better than I expected, I really hoped so. But it's not. It's actually worse. I don't even know what to say. Once you get back to … *normal*, you'll realise how insane this all is.'

'I'm sorry,' she said. 'I understand your anger.'

He got up, leaning on the armrest. 'Not that *bull*shit, please.' He started to walk away, but turned back. 'Don't try to tell me that my son is allergic to me … That I'm the one who caused his reflux. That I'm the reason why he cries. That's … you're completely out of your goddamn mind, you know that. Being pregnant affected your brain. The hormones have destroyed your mind. Fucking bitch.'

It was as though a dragon flew up from his breast. It felt fantastic. Never before had he let himself go like this towards her, and now it didn't matter anymore. He had lost, and there was no longer any difference between the wasteland of the dreams and the reality that lay before him.

• • •

The strange thing, he realised later, was that after that, everything had just gone on. She put the vacuum stopper back on the wine bottle and the dishes in the machine, the plates with the plates and the glasses with the glasses, and he knelt in the pantry and sorted out Friso and Hunter's laundry. He called out, asking whether she had anything for the wash. She went upstairs and came back down, adding their clothing to the mix in the tub. He had never been able to keep his eyes off the inside of underwear: Ruth's clotted foam, his brother-in-law's brown stripes, and the imprint of his anus stamped firmly onto the textile. Now he was repulsed by the thought that Friso's molecules were sloshing about in the same water as their clothes, and took out everything that belonged to the three of them. This was, he realised, intolerance at the cellular level.

When he went into the bedroom to get his alarm clock, Morris started crying. Ruth snapped on the light and lifted him from his cot. She put him to the breast. Edward closed the door quietly behind him.

In the middle of the night, he pissed in the upstairs sink. In the darkness, he asked himself whether there was still some way out, a little crack in their new circumstances that would allow him return to his former life. So he lay there fretting, that night and in the nights which followed, in the silvery white light that fell through the skylight, its vague glow encompassing the rowing machine and the outlines of the movers' boxes. Sometimes he clearly heard her voice saying 'I don't know what got into me, I'm so sorry', after which, in his thoughts, he reclaimed his place in their bed and in their life—and with these fantasies he fell asleep.

In the days that followed, he noticed that Ruth had attuned herself to a functional kind of friendliness, rather like a receptionist or travel hostess. He responded with a neutrality that left him wondering how long he could keep this up before setting the house on fire and fleeing to the eastern shores of the Black Sea, to become a palm reader in the streets of Tbilisi and eat mandarin oranges by the river.

He lived like a pariah in his own home, but told himself that he was doing so only to give her time to come back to her senses and see the idiocy of her ways.

One evening, he fixed risotto, which she loved, albeit in little servings. He watched contentedly as she ate, and noted that, in any case, things *looked* the way they always had been.

'Dear Ruth,' he said a little later, as though reading a letter aloud, 'please listen to me. Try to listen with your old ears, the ears you had back before we had Morris. Why don't we go to a doctor and ask what he thinks? Whether he's ever encountered a situation in which a father made his child sick? A father whose mere *presence* made his child cry? If that exists, that kind of allergy, then there must be other cases of it, too. Let's look for a doctor, one we've never seen before, who can help us with this, because things can't go on like this any longer.'

But she shook her head and said: 'I can't take another doctor. Things are just getting a bit better with him; I see no reason at all to go to another doctor.'

'But what about this for a reason?' he said, louder than he'd intended. 'I'm sleeping in the attic, you're treating me like a pariah, I'm a stranger in my own home!'

'Well, then, that's the way it is for now,' she said. 'Morris's health comes first. Once he starts feeling better, we'll see.'

The woman with whom he had lived for seven years had carried this woman inside her, a woman he didn't know and whom he had never before caught a glimpse of—a rigid, dogmatic creature, capable of no mercy, sticking to the straight and the narrow.

She kept Morris away from him as much as possible, and his periodic outbursts of rage at this only steeled her in her decision. He was their child's malady, and it was wise to keep children away from maladies.

Funny, he thought, *how quickly you became used to another person's madness*. In the rare moments when he was allowed to hold Morris and play with him, he did his utmost to show that his son felt at ease with him. That was how he tried to refute her conviction, by adapting to it. His assimilation went so far that he now moved around the house only on stockinged feet and always spoke quietly: anything to rule himself out as the cause. He lived like a phantom, and he winced when the steps creaked beneath his weight. He adapted quickly to his life as an illness. But his assimilation, he thought, was actually just one huge admission of his guilt. That was how she must perceive it, as a loud *Yes, I am Morris's sickness.*

At night, through the floor, he could hear him crying. Had he not wanted him, the way she said? He tried to get through to his thoughts and feelings from back then. When she'd said she was going to stop taking the Pill, he had agreed right away. He had been opposed to the fertility test, that was true, but did that mean he actually didn't want a child? Or did she regard even his half-mordant seed as *sabotage?*

The ultimate consequence of her thinking, he thought, as sleep went on eluding him, was that the sickness had to leave the house. She had not gone so far as to say it, but that could happen any moment.

In fact, he thought a while later, they *both* had the feeling that he should leave the house. She, so that their child could be healed; he, so that he could prove that his doing so had no effect on the baby's health. He would demonstrate his innocence. That would be his strategy, so that one day he could leave his life as illness behind him and become a father and husband once again. Yes, it would be better for everyone if he dropped out of sight for a while.

• • •

What a mistake to think that the world belongs to you as soon as you pull the front door closed behind you, toss your sleeping bag and carryall into the back of the car, and drive down the street. For Edward Landauer, the world actually grew smaller than ever. He now spent almost all his time at the institute, in his office. His backlog of work vanished quickly, his final lectures for that trimester were ready to go, and he just sat there, cruising the Internet. The listless surfing from here to there left him beside himself with disgust and boredom, but there was nothing else to do. At the end of the day, he left the building with the others, but returned after having dinner at The Wall of China. He took a doggy bag with him, in case he got hungry at night.

It was late June, a wall of green had thrown itself up around the institute.

'And,' Mrs. Hordijk, his secretary, asked, 'what are your plans for the summer vacation?'

'First a week at Juan-les-Pins,' he said. 'And after that, we'll see.'

'Lovely, isn't it, to just travel around and see where you end up?'

He nodded, yes, it was lovely—something like that.

In the evenings, he wandered through his staff's deserted offices. He examined photos of their families, and read their memos and the comic strips and pearls of wisdom they had cut out of the newspaper and hung on the wall. If they had forgotten to turn off their computers, he helped himself to their e-mails. And while they lay snuggled up against their partners in their peaceful homes, he snuck through their existences and wove together the loose ends of their unremarkable lives. Sometimes, before going to sleep, he would go by the animals, past the ferrets lying together in a tangle and, on their roosts, the chickens that opened one sleepy, beady little eye when he said 'Goodnight'. Returning to his office, he went to the cupboard where he kept his bedtime items: a sleeping bag, a self-inflating air mattress, and a down pillow from home. There, where the light came latest in the morning, in a corner under the windowsill, he made his bed. Above the little sink in the restroom, he brushed his teeth and trimmed his beard. On occasion, he showered under the emergency shower in a lab, because odours and signs of neglect might make people wonder.

In the hours that he lay awake, he returned to his early childhood, and remembered more and more of it all the time. At a certain point, in his mind's eye, his grandparents' orchard reappeared, bringing with it the sweet taste of sandhill plums and burgeoning, rust-dotted pears. It was a memory from the early 1960s, he calculated, before Route 59 had turned into the highway that put an end to the trees and the little farm itself and also—as his mother, for one, was firmly convinced—to his grandfather's life. Despondency, his father believed, didn't give one cancer, but his mother dipped into her ready supply of proverbs and adages, and pulled out this one: 'Not everything that can be counted counts, Willy, and not everything that counts can be counted.'

And so Edward climbed up and down the ladder of his life, and understood as little of the parts as he did of the whole.

One night, he was rudely awakened from his dozing. The door of his office flew open, and the light clicked on. Edward sat up partway and squinted. In the doorway stood a security guard. He took a few steps into the office, his hand on his hip, feeling for the flashlight that was big enough to serve as a club. His gaze swept over the man in front of him, and his bulging carryall. 'Who are you?' he said at last. 'What are you doing here?'

Edward pulled his pass from his pants pocket and handed it to him. The guard looked back and forth between the magnetic card and the man who was sitting in front of him, sticking out of his sleeping bag like a butterfly that had wriggled its way only halfway out of its cocoon.

'I'm the boss here,' Edward said.

'Maybe you are,' the other said. 'But still, what are you doing here at this hour?' The collar of his shirt was too wide for him; his neck stuck out a bit helplessly.

'Working overtime,' Edward said. 'Consider this overtime. And now I'd like to go back to sleep again, if you don't mind.'

'I'm only doing my job, sir.'

Since when were security guards so quick to take umbrage? So *indignant*?

He lay back down again and said: 'Tomorrow's going to be a long day. Please turn off the light.'

A few seconds later, Edward heard the footsteps retreating down the corridor. Sleep came as noiselessly as a scythe through the tall grass.

That weekend, he thought he was going to die of boredom. Marjolein was not answering the phone. He took a long walk in the woods around the institute. Beneath the light-green awnings of beech there hung a vague smell of rotting. He missed Morris, but it wasn't time for that yet; he had to be patient. Another two weeks, for sure. Mid-July, that was his guess—by that time she would have seen the error of her ways. It couldn't take longer than that. That wasn't possible.

Early that evening, he tried Marjolein's number again. 'Hello?' she said, in a tone that sounded as though someone else had picked up the phone for her.

'It's me,' he said.

'I can't talk right now,' she said hurriedly. 'I'll call you later.'

'That's fine, doll, sure,' he said, but she had already hung up.

He kicked the leg of his desk. Maybe her marine had come home. Where were the roadside explosive devices when you really needed them?

Sunday lay before him like a steep climb. He left the institute only to go to the supermarket. Because the one in Bilthoven was closed on Sundays, he had to drive into downtown Utrecht. The whole country smelled of suntan lotion; he snuck up and down the aisles like an illegal alien. He didn't want to run into any of his students. Merely a 'hello' would betray his miserable state. He drove back to the institute and put a few bottles of beer in the fridge of the kitchenette down the hall. The cool of the woods came in through the open window; at night, he sometimes heard owls.

Another six hours or so, then he could go to sleep. He longed for a message from home; he was deeply disappointed that Ruth didn't call. Like an exile, he was carried by the hour further and further from home, across rivers and plains, to the edge of the world where the sun never set. The mute darkness of evening was hardest to take, and so, in order to have those hours behind him as quickly as possible, he waited till late to walk to The Wall of China. But the restaurant was crowded, and he didn't feel like sitting at a table by himself amid all the cheerful cackling. The staff was friendly and discreet, the boy at the takeout counter said something like 'You like much Chinese food, right?', but that was it. He drank a beer and flipped through a few back issues of *Car and Driver*. Carrying his dinner in a plastic bag, he walked back to the institute.

He ate fried rice and vegetables. His phone did not ring—as though he were dead to the world.

• • •

Monday morning. Voices in the hallway, doors opening and closing. He listened with relief to the sound of life returning.

'Well, good morning,' Mrs. Hordijk said. 'You're in bright and early.'

He peeked into the lab where Marjolein usually worked. She wasn't in yet.

At the end of that morning's departmental meeting, Gerson stuck his grey head around the corner and said: 'Good morning, everyone. Don't let me interrupt you. Ed, when you're done, could I talk to you for a minute?'

'We've already finished,' Edward said.

They crossed the hall to his office. Gerson put his nose in the air, sniffed, and said: 'Man, what a smell. Are you starting a restaurant or something?'

He closed the door behind them and perched one

buttock on the edge of the desk. 'Listen, Ed ...'

Rolling his chair back from the desk, Edward looked up at him with an amused smile.

'How are you getting along?' Gerson asked.

Edward crossed his legs and leaned back in his chair. 'You've never asked me that before.'

'I'm serious, Ed.'

The smile slid from his face. 'Why do you ask? Is there anything wrong?'

Gerson looked him over. 'Two things,' he said. 'Or three, really. Your performance on the radio a while back, that wasn't very ... adept, to put it mildly. That's not the Ed I know.'

Edward coughed into his fist. Avoidance behaviour. 'What can I say,' he said. 'You know, with Morris ... it's very difficult. He still sleeps poorly, we're up all night with him. Maybe I'm not very sharp at the moment, that's right, but he'll be six months old soon, then the worst of it should sort of be behind us, then ...'

Talk, talk, keep talking. Cover everything with words, smother it.

'I suppose that's what's to blame.'

'And I hear that you've been sleeping in the office,' Gerson said, as though he hadn't been listening at all.

Don't flinch, don't give up. 'Oh, that time,' he said.

'It seems to me that you know that's not done. It gives people, how shall I put it, the wrong idea.' He looked around the office. 'Do you mind my asking why you sleep here?'

Edward started, stopped, began anew. 'I spend the night here sometimes, that's right. The rare occasion. When I've been working late. At home, it's ... I don't think you know what that's like, a child who cries all the time. Sleep deprivation is torture. So ... I know it's not exactly *de rigueur*, but Christ, under the circumstances ...'

'And are things okay at home otherwise? With Ruth? With the two of you?'

Edward scratched his arm with a pen. A grimace. 'Ups and down, of course, but these are tough times with Morris and all, like I said ... But otherwise, fine, yes.'

'Are you sure? If there's a problem, I can take that into account. I can cut you a little slack.'

'That's ... thanks, but it won't be necessary. Things are fine otherwise.'

'I don't want you sleeping here anymore, Ed. We can't have that.'

Edward nodded. He wished Gerson would wipe that look off his face. That surgical look. Were they done yet? Had he run through his little list? A wisp of rage spiralled up inside him. He was going to turn fifty next year, goddamn it; he didn't want to feel like this anymore. It was humiliating.

'One more thing,' Gerson said guardedly. He tilted his head back slightly, and perused him the way one

peruses the label on a bottle of wine. 'I don't know …
but I want to put an end to all the talk. That girl in your
department, Marjolein van Unen …'

His skin was an ill-fitting coat that tried to cover up
shock and shame. The bastard, he'd saved the worst for
last.

'I have … let's say I have fairly strong indications that
your relationship with her has not always been of a purely
professional nature.' He ran a hand over his forehead. 'I'd
like to hear you say it's not true. Please, Ed, convince me.
Otherwise we've got a problem.'

*No hesitation. Straight for the jugular. The paratrooper
in action.* Edward jabbed his arm with the tip of the
pen, there where it itched. He squeezed off a little laugh.
'Where do you get that?'

His words flapped through the room on fleshy,
cumbersome wings. Gerson took off his glasses and
twiddled them between thumb and forefinger. Arrogant,
tiresome, that's what they said about him, but he was
almost always right, and that was the least bearable trait
of all.

Edward's tongue was thick and dry in his mouth
when he said: 'God, Jaap, you know how people in the
department are always talking.'

He felt the urge to float out of there through the
open window, like a bit of willow fluff.

'This is serious, Ed. So I'm going to ask you one more

time: did you go off bounds with that girl?'

The crossroads. Further denial was dishonourable, unmanly, and somehow this wasn't the day for an even greater defeat. He knew he was digging his own grave, but he began nodding, hesitantly at first and then with increasing conviction, defending the last bit of honour he possessed. And also affirming a triumph—her young skin on his, the secret between her legs … 'Yes,' he said. 'Yes, Marjolein and I, we … well, fill in the rest.'

Gerson's lips curled in a frown. His breathing was audible. 'Jesus, Ed, that's … bad news. Bad news.'

Edward raised his hands and shrugged. What could he say?

'The code of conduct … You know how strict we are about that here.' He shook his head. 'I can't do anything but … treat this very seriously. I'm sorry.'

'I understand,' Edward said.

Gerson leaned forward, empathic now. 'It's not that I don't *understand*, Ed, it's really not that. I'm human, too. But this kind of thing … I can't just sweep it under the rug, you understand? The integrity of our department heads *has* to be above reproach …'

'Do what you have to do,' Edward said. He stood up and walked to the window. The seat of his trousers was sticking to his backside. His car was parked somewhere at the front of the lot. The sun was beating down on the roofs; the morning was clear and clean. If you felt like it, you could drive all the way to Vladivostok. On a morning like this, you could stand and look out over the Sea of Japan. Why did so few people do that, anyway?

Behind him, Gerson had risen to his feet. 'It's almost time for the summer break,' he said. 'Take your family down to France, find a quiet spot, and relax for a few weeks.'

'And what if I don't want to do that?' Edward turned around. 'I have research underway—I can't go away now.'

The little smile said it all. 'It's not a matter of wanting, Ed.'

Edward nodded resignedly. 'That's all I needed to know.'

Gerson held out his hand, and Edward automatically reached out to him, but Gerson said: 'The other one, please.' He took him by the left wrist and put his face down close to his forearm. He slid his glasses up onto his forehead. 'Sorry,' he said, 'it's the general practitioner in me.' He looked up. 'You've got ringworm, did you know that? Be careful around the baby—it's highly contagious.'

He waited till lunchtime before crossing the hall to the elevator. He walked to the parking lot with his bag and his bundle of bedclothes, and didn't look back.

At an intersection not far from the institute he parked the car and put his seat back. He slept for an hour and waited for three more, during which time he tried to oversee the scope of the catastrophe. All he could grasp were individual sentences, intonations … *Please, Ed, convince me …*

At five o'clock, he saw Marjolein's SEAT Ibiza turn into the street. He followed her at a discreet distance. She drove hard, jerkily, never using her turn signals. She turned onto the highway. It was funny, he thought, that when you started acting like a psychopath, you immediately felt like one, too. Marjolein took the same route that his own GPS dictated, and parked close to her house. He pulled up onto the curb a little ways behind her. Just as she was getting ready to climb out, he opened the passenger door and plopped down on the seat beside her.

'Fucking hell, Ed … I almost died …' Her hand on her heart.

She closed the door again and looked at him. She was holding her purse clutched to her stomach. He saw a vein pounding on the side of her neck. 'Why didn't you return my calls?' he said.

You also started sounding like a psychopath.

'Why are you here?' she said. 'What's going on?'

He looked through the windshield. The heat lay on the street, panting like a dog. The shoddy shops, the kerchiefs, the disgust on the boys' faces—like a street in Tangiers. He had been there once. The hard, impenetrable lives of Moroccans; everything there depressed him. 'Jaap knows,' he said. 'About us. He knows about it.'

'Fuck.'

He turned to her. 'Did you tell anyone?'

'What do you think?'

He flinched; his face looked as though he'd crumpled it. 'He'll be coming to you, too.'

She searched for something in her bag, and then saw the key in the ignition and took it out. 'What do you want me to do? What am I supposed to say?'

'I can't decide that for you … It probably won't go so badly for you.' He scratched his arm and said: 'I'm the one who's responsible.'

'You think so?' she said without looking at him.

'There's no need to worry.' He paused for a moment, and then said: 'How did he find out, Marjolein?'

Her hands, white and bony, gripped the wheel. Occasionally, someone glanced at them as they passed by. What did they see? A father and a daughter? A man and his mistress? Only people with problems sat in a car like this.

He looked at her. She shook her head. He would never touch her again, not like that; it was over. They had awakened from the dream; everything that was going on lay before them in the old, exhausted afternoon light.

He climbed out and walked to his car. As he drove past, she gestured to him. He stopped, and the window on the passenger side slid open. And there, on the hot asphalt, with the car door between them, she gave him her farewell present. She said: 'My phone was on the table. He picked it up. He saw it was you. Then he knew.' Her hand was on the doorsill, her eyes looking away through the windshield. 'That's how it went.'

He felt the vertigo of the duped. 'And "he" being?'

'Arrival at destination,' said the electronic voice.

'Jaap,' she said. She pulled her purse strap up higher onto her bare, brown shoulder. 'I'm sorry.'

• • •

He crossed the campground like a prisoner returning from war. Blue shadows flowed from between the tents; the start of the deluge.

'There's Uncle Ed!' Hunter shouted.

Edward put down his bag. With a smile that broke his face to pieces, he said: 'I've come to visit for a couple of days. Is that okay?'

'*Mi casa es tu casa*,' Friso said.

Edward cleared off the unused upper bunk and slid his bag under the bed.

'What's up?' Friso said from the doorway. 'Hassles at home?'

Edward nodded, his stiffened jaws prevented him from speaking.

A little later, as Friso was filling two cups with red

116

wine from a carton, he said: '*Il faut être toujours ivre.*
Upsy-daisy!'

Edward sat on the porch and drank tangy wine.
Mosquitoes bounced off his ears. You could hear the
hum of the highway; it was getting dark quickly now.
Hunter came back from the lavatories, which were lit up
in the distance like a service station. There was a stripe
of toothpaste on his lower lip. 'Good night, Uncle Ed.'

'Sleep tight, buddy.'

'Will you still be here early in the morning?'

'Yeah, I'm going to sleep there, in the bed next to
yours.' He pointed.

'And Morris and Aunt Ruth, too?'

'No. They're going to sleep nice and warm in their
own beds.'

The boy nodded contentedly.

When Edward had emptied his cup, he said: 'Guess
I'll turn in, too.' The sky glowed with the bundled light
of the city, flaring orange like fire. He remained seated.
Friso refilled their cups.

'I've made a complete mess of things,' Edward
mumbled, the first sentence of a letter never finished.
Friso said nothing, and Edward felt a trace of sympathy
for him, for his discretion, because he knew what it was
like to lose everything.

The night was filled with mosquitoes and demons.
He yearned for morning. At three-thirty he climbed

down the ladder and poked his brother-in-law, who was snoring. It was almost light outside by the time he fell asleep.

He drank instant coffee in the sharp-cut, early light of day. He had forgotten how fresh and pleasant it could be outside in the early morning. The little spider webs between the blades of grass were glistening and heavy with dew.

Later he shuffled off to the lavatories like a real camper, a roll of toilet paper in his hand. The day lay directionless before him. He had one lecture in the afternoon, that was all, the last one before the summer break. It would take an effort far beyond his own strength, but appearances were there to be kept up, like a hobo brushing his teeth beside a fountain.

That afternoon, he rented a bike at the reception desk and cycled to De Uithof. The complex of roads twisted and turned above the bike tunnels; he couldn't remember the last time he had ridden a bicycle. To his left, a park exhaled its coolness, and as he passed a vast graveyard among the greenery, he remembered the hen he had cared for when he was sixteen. He had taken it home as a tousled, yellow chick from a poultry farm outside the village. The farmer had let him do it, indifferently, knowing how it would end. Edward wanted to give it a good life amid the brood of bantams in the yard. The chick grew to become a big, passive chicken, barely inclined to move, and despite its size soon fell victim to the keen little hens that chased it around the garden and picked out its white feathers. He couldn't protect it from the covey's aggression, and had the feeling that he was witnessing two defeats. That of the chicken, which was ostensibly failing to *make good*, and his own: he had wanted to do something benevolent, and it had resulted in an indisputable fiasco. The hen was designed for a lifespan of about six weeks, and in fact seemed resigned to that. He felt a bit of hatred for the submissive, malformed creature, and was ashamed of that hatred.

Somewhere in his early days at college, the chicken must have died. He had no idea what his parents had done with the dead bird, his chicken, which he had forgotten about completely until this day on which his memories unfurled before him, clear and colourful. He couldn't imagine why he had failed to come up with that chicken during his discussions with Ruth, when she accused him of being unfeeling — the distinct volumes of his biography somehow refused to merge into a whole, a single life possessed of meaning and coherence.

The auditorium was barely half-full. It was the day before summer break. The windows were open. When the stumping around was over and the voices stilled, he said:

'Once I had a white chicken. She was born in a hatchery somewhere and grew up in a warm shed with thousands, tens of thousands, of others like herself. When we talk about growing up here, of course, we're talking about something quite different from the gradual process of cell division that you refer to as your youth, and which you took twenty years to complete. No, she was bursting at the seams after about six weeks on a diet of concentrate and antibiotics, from a few grams to around one-and-a-half kilos in six weeks, an Olympian achievement ... Imagine if you would that you were to grow up among your own contemporaries, without parents, grandparents, uncles, aunts ... Everywhere you look, only people of your own age, rather like those festivals you people attend ...'

He heard laughter, shouts of affirmation.

'It was in that shed that I found her,' he said, 'my fattened chick, almost six weeks old and ripe for the slaughter, atop a thick paddy of excrement —'

'Lowlands!' a boy at the back shouted. Laughter rolled from the rows of seats.

'I picked her up just like that,' he went on, 'and I don't know why, but I decided that I was going to rescue this one chicken.' He looked into the auditorium from over the tops of his reading glasses. 'Had I possessed the language to explain to her what "mother" meant, she still would not have understood me. In her world, there was nothing to be found that pointed in that direction.

When I took her out of the shed and gave her a life amid the other chickens in our backyard, there was no way I could have known that it would be impossible for her to live with the others, who were all socialised.' He raised his hands. 'And so I bestowed upon my chicken a life even less happy than the one she already had, out of *idealism*. And so I also extended that life beyond the limits of the bearable ...'

He stopped for a moment to wipe the sweat from his forehead. 'The important thing,' he went on, 'is that you have heard me use the words "less happy". My chicken, I have said, was unhappy. She did not know how to live among members of her own species, other birds who did know how to do that, how to be chickens. In our circles, it is not common to talk about the feelings of animals. We don't deny that animals might have feelings, but we also don't acknowledge that they might have them. We stick to the comfortable mean, which my wife claims is an indication of a defective moral sense.'

Some of the students were still busy taking notes, he saw. Such touching industry. His thoughts began to wander; he had no idea how he could proceed from the story of his chicken to the subject of this lecture, which was vectors, and the conditions under which H5N1 could become airborne.

'This afternoon,' he said with his eyes closed, 'while cycling here, I thought for the first time in ... thirty,

thirty-five years about that chicken, and was surprised to find that I had truly *loved* her, for a while. Or in any case … that I possessed something like *compassion* … When I go into a hatchery these days, all I want is to get out again as quickly as possible. The ammonia fumes make your eyes burn, you almost can't catch your breath. In fact, I rarely think these days about the animals that are born, grow up, and die under such conditions. All I think is: how soon can I get out of here? In that way, and I believe that is what I am trying to say this afternoon, I differ from that boy with his chicken. That is, I am … a different person.'

He grasped the edges of the lectern.

'Something has happened in the meantime … something irreversible. That's the way it goes, unfortunately, as we grow older … we lose a certain sort of sensitivity. Our receptors become numbed. That is why old age is unbearable, because you sometimes suddenly remember what it was like … to have a *heart*, a heart that made you capable of great, rash deeds, to be caught up and feel a part of life on earth …'

He looked up. The last of the pens had stopped writing.

'Am I getting side-tracked?' He took off his glasses and wiped them on the shirttail hanging from his trousers. 'To have a heart,' he said, wiping in concentration, 'that could make you happy or unhappy, and that even linked you to something like a *chicken* … A chicken, for God's sake. A white chicken.' He held his hands apart, to indicate the size.

'In neurology, there is a term for what I'm talking about,' he said after a few seconds. '*Anesthesia dolorosa* … painful numbness.'

He looked into the auditorium. It was a blur.

'Thus far, my introduction … I believe …' He folded his glasses and placed them on the papers in front of him. He heard shuffling, whispering, like in a church. He wiped his forearm across his eyes, but they kept running over. He tried not to make a sound, but couldn't stop himself from sniffing loudly. Vague forms began moving towards the exit.

'Sir?' a girl said. He waved her away. The auditorium emptied, and at the exit a few students stood and stared at the weeping man on the podium, until they, too, entered the hallway and disappeared, on their way into the summer.